# MICHAEL KENT PUBLICATIONS

## NOVELS

**-THE BIG JIGGETY (Xlibris, 2005)**
**-POP THE PLUG (Xlibris, 2012)**
**-ALL OF THE NIGHT (Xlibris, 2015)**

## SHORT STORIES

-Looking for Annie Oakley (Paris, Ed. Fernand Nathan, '87--revised '97)
-Basement Boon (Los Angeles, Fiction Forum, Dec. '92)
-Merlot in the Shower (L.A. Fiction Forum, Dec. '93)
-Rock Around the Clock (Writer's Round Table [McHenry, MD], April '97)
-Geller Pushes his Luck (Writer's Round Table, June '97)
-The Phone Call (Happy 10, '98, NYC)
-Cinema Rumania (Threshold, Winter '98-'99, Vol.3, Issue 2, Pittsburgh)
-To Keep One's Shirt On (Threshold, Fall '99, Vol 3, issue 2)
-American Conversation (Happy 15, 2000)
-The Turn of the Key (Threshold, 2000)
-The Piano Boy (Inostrania Literatura, Moscow, Aug. 2008)

## POETRY/SONGS

-Three poems in the **Bowdoin Quill** (+ illustrations and photos) '79-'80
**-LES MALEFICES DU FARDEAU D'ATLAS**, a collection of early
    poems ('74-'80), Éditions Saint-Germain-des-Prés, Paris ('85)
-ICE DON'T FLOAT IN DIRTY WATER (Road Publishers, Palmyra,
    Virginia) '97
-The BALLAD OF MIKE & LOLO + AROUND THE CORNER, (Road
    Publishers '98, Vol. 15)
-DAGUERREOTYPE (Road Publishers '99, Vol. 16)
-THE CANARY & THE PEACH (Poetry.com, June 2000)
-RETURN + JULIA (Road Publishers 2000, Vol. 17)
-JUST TWO (Road Publishers 2001, Vol. 18)
-WRINKLES, HARD DISCUS, QUARTERED (Road Publishers 2002,
    Vol. 19)

## TEXTBOOK

-**VOIE EXPRESS USA** ('87, revised '97) C.L.E./Fernand Nathan, Paris
Includes 20 chronicles and a four chapter novella "Looking for Annie
Oakley"
-**INGLES POR LA VIA RAPIDA** ('92) Larousse/Barron's. Spanish
Version of Voie Express

## ARTWORK

-Several Cartoons, published on a regular basis in **The Bowdoin Sun**
(1977-78, Brunswick, ME)
-Illustrations & photographs, published in **The Bowdoin Quill** ('79-'80)
-"NY Sidewalk Flowershop," published in the Bowdoin collection "No
Cats No Steeples" ('80)
-Painting ("Still Life & Seascape") published by The Encyclopedia of
Living Artists ('86)
-Photo in anti-alcohol Canadian publication ('81)
-Illustrations for the Foreign Service Institute's French textbook (1985;
Arlington, VA)
-Several Cartoons (8), published on a monthly basis, by The Columbia
Road Magazine ('85-'87, Washington, DC)
-Painting ("Still Life & Seascape") published by The Encyclopedia of
Living Artists ('86)
-Photo of *Le Monde* correspondent Henri Pierre published in **France-
Amérique** ('87)
-Caricature of Pdt. Pompidou published in the **Alexandria Gazette-Packet**
('88, Alexandria, VA)
-Two Photos (Latin America & Eastern Europe) published in The World
Bank's **The Urban Age** (May '96)
-Three illustrations published in **Kinesis** (April '97)
-Painting ("L'âme espagnole") **Happy** '97
-Painting ("Bicyclist in Amsterdam") in the December 1999 Bulletin of
the Alliance française of Washington, DC
-Hitchhiker on *The Big Jiggety* Novel (Dec. '05)
-Washington Project for the Arts/WPA Catalogue (Sept. 08)
-Several Paintings featured in **Downtown L.A. Life Magazine**

-Reproduction of Picasso work/**Downtowner** - 2010
-Paintings and photos in *Pop the Plug* (2012)
-Paintings, drawings, and photos in *All of the Night* (2015)

## NEWSPAPER ARTICLES (features, humor columns, music-film-theater reviews, etc)

-From **The Bowdoin Sun** to **The Takoma Voice**, onward ('78-90)(161 articles)
[includes **The Alexandria Gazette, The Vineyard Gazette, The Springfield Independent, The Burke Herald, The Fairfax Tribune, The Columbia Road Magazine, The Alexandria Port-Packet, The Washington Post, The Gloucester Daily Times**]
Detailed list available upon request

# All of the Night

*Novel No. 3 An Albert Nostran Episode*

## Michael Kent

**Images by Michael Kent**

Copyright © 2015 by Michael Kent.

| Library of Congress Control Number: | | 2015905690 |
|---|---|---|
| ISBN: | Hardcover | 978-1-5035-6167-0 |
| | Softcover | 978-1-5035-6169-4 |
| | eBook | 978-1-5035-6168-7 |

Print information available on the last page.

Rev. date: 05/14/2015

**To order additional copies of this book, contact:**
Xlibris
1-888-795-4274
www.Xlibris.com
Orders@Xlibris.com
711754

I would like to extend my thanks to my mother, Lois Kent, Lidia Terziotti and Ann O'Neal Garcia

## SOME OF THE CHARACTERS

Albert Nostran, Hero
Quentin Nostran, Father
Nina Nostran, Mother
Simon Nostran, Brother
Ferdinand Latulipe, friend
Dominique Mouluvert, boss
Pierre Hertzen, editor-in-chief
Achilles Pétard, sub-editor
Benoit Joffre, sub-editor
Hervé Douanel, sub-editor
Davey Gronket, housemate
Gloria, friendly lass
Jillian, a museum attendee
Deborah, mirage
Claire M., copy-girl
Carl, landlord
Flora, landlordess
Lily, housemate
Darwell, Supervisor
Ramona Mendez, Office Manager
Fred Gulan, journalist
Sandra, executive secretary

Balthazar, a car of the old world

## Ye Olden Gang

Gaspard Casard, Friend
Edouard Lessèphe, Friend, Drummer
Victor Ravin, Friend

# CONTENTS

## Part I

## Part II

*Part I*

# RONALD REAGAN'S

Although it was a couple of minutes before seven (post meridiem), Connecticut Avenue, one of the Capital City's main arteries, was already dead. And confusing. I was walking around in circles, or imperfect rectangles rather, trying to locate the ABC News building. It was there a second ago; now where? Mystery and gumball. This was infuriating. Not that I was particularly interested in *it*, but it would serve as a landmark. I was also surprised not to see CBS or NBC around the corner.

So, for the third time I walked up the smooth incline whose stately buildings — some of them, and the blonde Mayflower Hotel in particular certainly qualifies — and sporadic elms, were still lightly brushed by the late afternoon sun like in a Monet painting [1]. But no ABC building to be found; no opportunity to see the first three letters of the Roman alphabet or catch a peep of a famous anchorman, like Donald Samson, or woman, like... like..., but just bask in the fading ultraviolet rays or perhaps grab a bite to eat, because my stomach was beginning to feel empty. First death, then hunger.

To the left, past a store selling guitars, I spied a Ronald Reagan's, a food chain I had never heard of before I set foot in the District of Columbia. The name had from the start struck me as peculiar. I recall my first night wandering listlessly up Pennsylvania Avenue from George Washington University past a triangle of grass, trees, bushes, and benches, and seeing "Ronald Reagan's Family Restaurant."

I avoided it. The word "family" scared me away. It sounded as though it would be expensive, and I was not sure whether I had secured the job at the Universal Wire Service. The world-renowned U.W.S.

---

1    One would prefer alluding to an artist of lesser renown, but Monet just fits the mood.

They could have called the eatery Audie Murphy, or chosen among the dozens of famous cowboys, or actors, or actors playing cowboys. Roy Rogers would have been good. Although one assumes the jolly chap not to be exactly left of center, there is a less political ring to it than "Ronald Reagan," the actor turned governor of California and now in the final leg of the presidential race, the results of which were around the corner. Like the restaurant.

Of course, Washington, D.C. is the American political city par excellence, perhaps the only political city in the nation — which is odd when you know that the United States is a federation and a democracy, and politics should at least be occurring in 50 places simultaneously, not to mention the municipal and county levels and the minds of 240-million-odd concerned citizens.

Ronald Reagan's. Really. It did not quite sound serious. Lord knows my ex-roommate Jake hated him; so, as a result I felt obligated to somewhat take the opposite side. Anyway, was the man in charge that good? Jimmy?

Sure, there had been Camp David. The Israelis and the Egyptians had embraced. Namely Sadat and little Begin. But what about the helicopters that had crashed in the Iranian sand? And the 52 hostages? The 52 American hostages imprisoned in Tehran! My god they were driving me crazy! The way Wally Krankheit[2] at CBS rubbed it in every night!

"And that's the way it is, November 2nd, 1980, 404 billionth day for the American hostages in Iran." They are no longer young, no longer sane, but, gosh, they are American.

With William Randolph Hearst it had been: "Remember the Maine, remember the Maine!" Hearst had sent a photographer down to Cuba to see what the evil — or need it be specified? — Spaniards were up to, and when his man had said "Not much," Hearst had purportedly responded, "Please remain. You furnish the pictures, and I'll furnish the war."

So what were old, good-natured, mustachioed Wally and his brethren up to anyway? Reminding us of Jimmy's incompetence, fuel the resentment of the people, make Ronnie a shoe-in? How about all the other things going on in the world? I wondered, stepping on to

---

2    -Illness, in German.

the fast-food restaurant's red-tiled floor which glowed from its most recent mopping.

Did Reagan himself own this restaurant? I did not know and I did not want to know. Which is a shameful attitude for an aspiring journalist, but hunger is like love; it does not seek to find out too much before the itch has been sufficiently scratched.

"What'll it be?" a young fellow in a yellow plastic cowboy hat and a vermilion shirt asked, when I presented myself in front of the counter. Very polite in a styrofoam sort of way.

"A shoe-sole burgermeister, Zen fries, and a tooth-melter."

"SHOE-SOLE, ZENS, MELTER!" he screamed while still staring me in the face with pale green eyes while I looked down at his fingers punching the secret code. Nice college ring, dude.

After thanking him profusely — was he not responsible for the end of this ordeal? I am not one to take matters for granted — I looked around. The place was curiously packed. Or should I say, furiously? So this is where Washingtonians hang out when all is said and done? Or rather done, because there was a little bit of saying materializing before my very ears as the conversations seemed to testify. I did find a table next to the window overlooking a Guggenheim shoe store, famous for its inwardly spiraling moccasins. Suddenly I felt like having escargots.

Instead, I had started to bite into my burgermeister when I heard a voice talking to me.

"Do you mind if I join you?"

A timid, feminine voice. Jesus. Or rather, Gloria.

Contrary to what I had assumed earlier, the restaurant was virtually empty. I looked up to see a young woman in her mid-twenties but more of a late twenties attitude, a certain apprehension that appears to come with age and tenses certain facial muscles, namely around the forehead and the mouth. She gazed at me, as much as one hates to write such things, with wide blue eyes, but that was the color, and a pretty one too.

"Shure," I replied, not meaning to misspell the word but attempting to convey that my mouth still contained a little chunk of the burgermeister.

*

# GROUCHO DENVER

"You know what?"

"Tell me."

"You look like a combination of John Denver and Groucho Marx," she said, reassuring me since one of my secret fears was that I did not look like anyone famous. I grunted a response.

"Shlick."

"Yes. John Denver for the high cheekbones, the metal-rimmed glasses — of course you weren't born with those — and Groucho around the eyebrows and the eyes."

"I was born with those."

"Ha-ha-ha. It's like a combination of innocence and..."

Perversion? Guile? I wondered silently while attacking the fries on which I had squeezed a little horseradish sauce. A small paper container of mayonnaise waited on the far right corner of my tray just in case.

"No. Savvy, wit. Something like that."

She took a nibble out of her perfectly feathered chicken breast. Sandwich. I sipped on the tooth-melter. As usual there was too much ice. Such a rip-off! But it soon melted. And the brown turned to amber.

"Did you vote?" I asked her.

"Yes, and you?"

"Sure did. It's a citizen's duty."

"Indeed. May I ask for whom?"

I looked at her short slightly wavy dark brown hair, her grey-green office attire, into her watery blue eyes.

"John Anderson."

The third party candidate with the thick white hair, horn-rim spectacles and the Greek wife from whom Jane Fonda asked

Democrats to stay away so that we could enjoy four more years of Carter.

"You did? So did I! But I don't think he'll get in; Americans don't like third-party candidates and he's really been sliding in the polls."

"You never can tell until the last minute."

She tilted her head; a drop of ketchup landed on her blouse.

"I hope you're right. Are you registered in D.C.?"

"No, in Massachusetts."

Her big eyes opened even wider.

"Wow, that's wild! I'm from Massachusetts too. Lawrence. And you?"

"Me? Stone Harbor."

"Oh, it's so pretty up there with all the painters and the ocean!"

"Too bad the town is dry."

She laughed, displaying a fine row of teeth, the kind dentists' nightmares are made of. Too much fluoride in the water these days.

When our dishes were but stringy remainders muddled in bright red and yellow sauces, I suggested, feeling most adult-like and not having any other plans, that we go somewhere else for a drink. A real one.

"Oh, oh, yes, that would be nice."

Her face seemed to stretch, become more gaunt. As she rose, I noticed that while she had a hint of a stoop, seemingly more due to shyness than scoliosis, she was quite tall, which I had not observed when we were sitting down. This meant that either her chair was lower than mine, that she slouched — although I had not noticed it — or she had very long legs. She was not even wearing any high heels. Sneakers, I'm afraid.

We walked up Connecticut Avenue, Northwest's mild incline up to Dupont Circle. Aside from the Poplar Drugstore, the place was dead. Although I had never visited this area before, it struck me as more quiet than normal. More quiet than this rather attractive, turn-of-the century neighborhood should be. Once again, I was taken by the feeling of emptiness that had struck me when I first got off the Boston train at Union Station.

"It's a weekday," the tall woman explained. Suddenly she seemed dismayed that I had in some ways criticized the city she had adopted to live in. I should not have commented on the vacuum I sensed; it seemed to make her aware of her own vulnerability, of the intrinsic imperfection of things against which she appeared to be struggling.

"Nice statue," I said as we passed the white-marbled center of the circle.

"Oh, yes. Normally, it's a fountain and people sit around the benches. Some play chess, others toss a Frisbee around, musicians bring out their guitars and their flutes, a lot just hang out. It's very pleasant during the day and when the sun is out."

It seemed as though she were trying to convince me that we were not in some kind of backwater town but in the vibrant capital of the United States of America.

"Is that a movie theater up the street?" I asked, spotting something resembling a marquee.

Part of me felt like saying: is this <u>the</u> movie theater? As though interpreting my thoughts, she said:

"Oh, but there are many others in the city."

"Actually, I seemed to notice one near the Ronald Reagan's."

"Oh, yes. I went there not too long ago. It plays a lot of good movies."

We passed a few restaurants then the first theater. "Taxi Driver" appeared in black bold letters.

"Have you seen it?" she asked as we entered a bar in which at least a few Washingtonians could be found, drinking beer and watching THE game, trying to look important, speaking rather loudly at times, but ultimately failing to be truly expressive or impressive. No John Denvers or Groucho Marxes in this crowd.

"Twice. It's a terrific film."

"Is it? I haven't seen a good movie in ages... By the way, where are you staying?"

"Well, my bags are still in a locker at the Youth Hostel, down on Eye Street, and er..."

"Hm. That's not a bad neighborhood, except for all the sleazy shows."

She laughed. I felt like slapping her on the back but perhaps that was premature.

The worst part is that the shows she was referring to are extremely unimaginative and boring. Not that I have seen any but one can imagine. The women are invariably total sluts who have a vocabulary of two words. Of course, one does not expect terribly high moral standards, little Mother Teresas of Calcutta in the raw, or garter-belted, prancing around with gold stiletto heels, kicking up pink pulsating legs, wagging a wholesome pair of knock-knock-come-ins, shaking steaming buttocks an inch or two away from one's eyeglasses; but, at least they could stretch their limited acting abilities and pretend, play a little bit harder to get. Nothing is quite as sexy as a woman saying "no, you shouldn't," while licking her chops, with moist eyes, quivering nostrils, and vibrating lips, implying "go ahead you animal, you." They never ever wear underwear and strip naked for the first stranger with enough meat to start a delicatessen in a couple of rushed seconds. As far as the men go, you do not expect the likes of Adlai Stevenson or Frank Lloyd Wright, but still a little braininess would give the films a bit of an edge, and, who knows, turn them into big box-office hits. Parents could bring their children... The possibilities are endless.

"You could come over to my house?" Gloria suggested.

My eyes did their best not to pop open. After putting my hand in front of them lest an eyeball escape I looked at her. She was still there gazing at her foot as it scraped the pavement.

"That sounds good."

"Sure. You seem like a nice guy."

But watch out for the Groucho Marx in me.

\*

# III

# GLORIA

Gloria hailed a taxi, a venerable black and orange Dodge Dart. Funny, New York is more a city of Chevrolets, here most of the cabs seem to be Chryslers. After slamming the creaking door shut, we plunged into the night down some hill into some kind of forest. Suddenly, Washington was getting more exciting. The question however remained: who was Hansel and who was Gretel around here? And first and foremost who was the witch? Well, if worse came to worst the taxi driver could save my life. Except of course if he was in cahoots. I had to examine all angles.

"This is Rock Creek Park," she said with a hint of pride permeating her voice, as though she had planted most of the trees or at least had landscaped a couple of acres.

The road twisted and turned. Swerved. The tires of the cars hissed on the pavement which had become wet since we had had our drink in the bar with a few Washingtonians watching THE game.

"It's beautiful," I blurted, "quite surrealistic to have such an expanse of green in the middle of a major city."

"Do you know it's almost 2,000 acres? The city acquired it at the end of the 19th century. Further north, there's the Carter Barron Amphitheater and there's a whole slew of nature walks, horse trails, picnic areas, sport facilities..."

Yeah, yeah.

"The cab doesn't have a meter," I remarked, so as to demonstrate that I was paying very close attention.

"Oh, in Washington fares are determined by the zones. See, you have a map which indicates what the zones are. It's a pretty good system although some of the drivers can take you literally for a ride."

We entered a long, neon-lit tunnel.

"But I'm not one of them!" the cabby chuckled up front, revealing a strong foreign accent.

"Where are you from?" I asked. I had to get to the bottom of this. And fast.

"Persia."

"Oh? Some of my ancestors come from Albion," I retorted.

"Albion? Where's that at?"

Marveling at how well he had adopted the lingo, I answered.

"Northwest of Persia. Actually, just north of Gaul and Batavia and East of Eire."

"Wow. You know your geography."

"I'm American, aren't I?" I responded, not overly embarrassed at the non-sequitur.

"Okay, you've arrived."

Outside, a faint drizzle had resumed, a solitary lamppost lit the street. Despite the obscurity and thick foliage I noticed a cluster of row-houses. The cab splashed away, gulped by the night.

"This is where I live," Gloria announced, returning to the surface. "God, you really had the driver going!"

"It's the Groucho aura."

"Ha-ha-ha," she genuinely giggled. "I live in the basement. I must warn you it's pretty small."

In that case I am leaving.

"I'm sure it's fine."

The adventure was tingling my skin. She turned on the light. The apartment was neither clean nor dirty, neither messy nor neat. A beige carpet with enough stains not to make it petit bourgeois covered the floor. In the back I could spot a few dishes still soaking. A sock or two had been tossed in various corners of the room without much forethought or forewarning.

"Well, this is it. Do you want anything to drink?"

I noticed that her feet no longer wore shoes.

"Sure."

"I don't have much. Er... just light beer, I'm afraid."

"Perfect for this time of night." If one is to believe the commercials.

*   *   *

We talked about looking for a job and finding one. She is temporarily employed as an editor at the Association for Retired Employees.

"It's pretty challenging."

Ah, if it's challenging, you've said it all.

"I'll bet."

"And you... er. I don't remember your name."

Because I never told you, you big silly.

"Nostran, Albert Nostran."

"It has a nice ring to it."

"My father is a writer."

"That's interesting. What do you do?"

"I am following a sort of internship at the Universal Wire Service."

"Oh, that sounds interesting. What do you do there?"

"Let me give you a glimpse of a typical day. Pierre Hertzen, the news director, fishes up some obscure story, either from the Associated Press or some arcane news release, which need or need not be treated, and asks me to see what I can come up with."

Gloria nods. She seems quite mesmerized, an unexpected hint of saliva dotting the corner of her mouth like a pearl earring.

"Then, I find a vacant desk, swivel the swivel-chair around up and down till it reaches a height suitable to me, settle down behind a massive typewriter which types using a shiny, inky, massive font, read over the material, synthesize it, translate the quotes..."

"Translate?"

"Oh, yes, I forgot to mention that this is a French press agency."

"French? Even though it's called the Universal Wire Service?"

"It's also known as *Le Service de Presse Universel*."

"It sounds so much more romantic that way. But I'm sorry, I interrupted what you were saying."

I nod, smile.

"After that, I pound away what I believe an acceptable dispatch to be, occasionally blowing a fuse or two..."

"I would imagine."

"Pff. Then I walk over to his desk..."

"Hertzen's?"

"Yes, inevitably I feel that I am interrupting something crucial, and show it to him."

"What does he do then? Just the way you talk, I can tell you are a writer."

Gloria, you are also one hell of an observer.

"He adjusts his bifocals on a nose that could have inspired a social-realist artist, proofreads the copy, butchering my original prose, and if the satellite, the lines or whatever, are not too busy I get to send it out. Once the story appears in minute green letters on the Video Display Terminal's screen, all that is required is to push the "send button: blip, and voilà. *Le tour est joué*[3]."

"Sounds fascinating."

"I must say that so far I am enjoying it a lot. The only problem..."

"The only problem?"

"Yes, the only problem..."

I look at her. Her knees are under her chin, a very adolescent pose for a woman who seems in other ways quite mature. I lose my train of thought but it then comes back to me.

"The problem is that, after the initial training is over, I'm going to have to work nights."

"Nights? Ouch. Yes that can be rough, but I assume that after a while you'll switch back to the daytime."

"That's why I was hired originally: to replace a man who was losing his sanity..."

"What are the exact hours?"

"Twelve midnight to eight o'clock in the morning. Not the greatest hours, probably the worst, but I was sick of the dead-end dishwashing job I held before. It had come to its seasonal close anyhow. I was also sick of my father yelling at me day in and day out, insulting me, digging in as far as he could since the family moved back to America."

"Where did you all live before?"

"Near Paris."

"That's where you picked up the French."

"Precisely. Anyhow, after my brother took off for Syracuse University, I hopped on a train southbound. Right now, the whole idea seems very abstract. A bridge to cross when I get to it."

"I think you have the right attitude."

She stares at me with those big watery blue eyes.

*

---

3   -The trick is done.

# IV

# CONNECTICUT, NORTHWEST

To make a long and not the most fascinating story in the world short, I ended up spending the night in her bed. You might argue, if this is not fascinating, what is? Perhaps; but, while I was enjoying her mattress, cotton sheets, and a riveting perspective of the low, slightly warped ceiling, she retreated to the sofa, three feet away from the most symbolic of partitions, insisting I be the more comfortable one; and, since I was not enthralled to press the issue I did not. A modernist, I do believe a man and a woman can just be friends. Contrary to what my college roommate Jake believed, I am not ready just to hop on the first person. Not only would this have been shooting fish in a bucket, I must confess that fish does not qualify exactly as my favorite dish.

After a rather nice cup of coffee, I bid tender Gloria goodbye.

"Let's get together again," she suggested.

"Oh yes. Definitely."

Did she seem a trifle disappointed or were my ego and paranoia getting the better of me?

A nice cool sun was whipping the brick-laid neighborhood. I sauntered down a flight of steps I had not noticed the night before. Whoever said Washington is flat must be crazy, for indeed here was another hill. A few cars were driving by so I stuck my thumb out. Soon, one of them stopped and gave me a ride down and up the hill again to Connecticut Avenue.

"Are we far from K Street?" I asked.

"Quite a ways. Unfortunately I'm not headed in that direction."

You turd, as my dear father would tell people.

"Which street is this?"

"Porter. Did you know that Rock Creek Park was..."

All of the Night

And he went on to tell me almost verbatim what Gloria enunciated last night before the evil deed did not occur.

Shortly after having been dropped off, I noticed a subway or Metro station emerging from the wide Connecticut Avenue sidewalk, next to a pizza parlor. A passerby, sporting a grey flannel suit and a fedora (trailing a couple of suspicious communists), informed me that it would be a good couple of years before I or anybody else could take a train from this location, which I found out was Cleveland Park. I would rather call that a bad couple of years.

I suppose I could have waited that long, but the job beckoned. I looked at my watch: 11 o'clock. My internship is in some respects a remarkably relaxed one, mind you; in theory I am making up my own schedule, still I feel compelled by a sense of duty to show up, to pose as a regular.

Quickening my pace I walk past the Uptown Movie Theater, the Calliope bookstore, an ice cream parlor, a post office, cross a bridge down below which Rock Creek meanders. A symphony of yellows and reds and branches dancing in all directions. To my left, after the two massive, fluted, cement jars which place a final punctuation mark on the bridge, I see a huge 1930s apartment complex where I read: Kennedy Warren, and the idea of assassination enters my mind. How odd, how all those political figures were shot in the sixties. Not only J.F.K. and his brother, but Malcolm X, Martin Luther King. Of course Gerald Ford almost got knocked off in the seventies; but, Lennon, corroborating what I told Jake up at Burdon, said he felt that a new era of peace and musical inspiration was around the corner. Amen.

Suddenly, I think of my father. Who, as a young man, looked like Lennon and perhaps James Joyce. I look down at the leaves and the tree trunks. My father who is not talking to me anymore since I left Stone Harbor. Well, Dad, I have a job now. I am not washing dishes anymore. As a matter of fact, I am following in your footsteps. I am employed as a journalist and if I make it past this first month, God knows what will happen. I clear my nose and throat and watch my spit spin down to the blanket of leaves down below.

The trek continues. In the middle of the street is the most extensive zebra crossing I have ever set eyes on and to the left: the National Zoo. That will be a good place to take a woman when I find one.

They seem quite friendly around here and there are a lot of them. All in good time.

The road slopes downward. To the right, beyond an ivy-blanketed gradient, the local Sheraton Hotel spreads its wings, which are as numerous as they are eclectic. From the Victorian age to the 1970s, somewhat unified or at least tied together, by ubiquitous red brick. I walk by another potential Metro station whose fate appears linked to Cleveland Park's. This one bears the name of Woodley Park/Zoo. In a couple of years I will metro with my woman to the zoo.

I cross a second bridge guarded by two emaciated lions, as though the sculptor wished to mitigate the sense of grandeur or ran out of cement. A procession of wing-flapping eagles, roosted on ionic columns painted a dubious light green, follows. Under the birds hang large glass balls, as though to attest to their masculinity, and which, one presumes, light up at night. Time has cracked the railing. The concrete sidewalk has been patched up here and there by asphalt. Weeds are growing wherever there are fissures; a beer bottle has been broken here not long ago, and then another one, and then a third; Hertzen, would you be interested in a scoop? I look down. My God, not you again. Rock Creek, you snake in the grass, you! Little cars are following the contours of the road, although it seems that from this distance their choice is arbitrary. You can do anything you want, cars, you are far away!

Connecticut Avenue swirls by the Chinese Embassy like a dragon practicing yoga, then past a series of tall, majestic, ornate turn-of-the-century edifices, one of which espouses the road's curvature before the latter takes a final plunge.

I am on the top of the hill and the sky is a cheerful baby blue while the sun is shining from its highest point, illuminating the rows of early twentieth century buildings down below as though they were etched out of ivory. With the Hilton, a half parenthesis of a building, a 1960s totalitarian half crescent which time has yet to grace. I think back on the Kennedy Warren and the Kennedy assassination, but I am distracted by the hustle and bustle of automobiles and pedestrians down below. All is well, Madame la Marquise. Life has returned. One block more and I am fully back into civilization. The neighborhood, which was more dead than an assassinated celebrity the night before, has reemerged.

A couple of blocks more and here is a third subway station. A subway station under which trains actually rumble and which enables me to accomplish the final leg of my journey down to Farragut North and K Street. K for karma, karisma, katalist, Jesus Krist, katch a wave. To think that I could still be in Stone Harbor right now! No, not I!

After a quick chicken salad sandwich with lettuce and tomato, eaten on a bench, admiring a pair of human breasts, I catch the elevator up to the Universal Wire's fourth floor. Walk through the door and greet the two secretaries who flash the kind of smile that would undoubtedly crack a Burdon College face.

*I AM NOT A GIRL, I AM A WOMAN!* I can still hear them screaming in my ears with dripping tray in hand waiting in line for the cafeteria line to move onward, and me looking out the window, pining for the pines to whisper in their ear to shut up. *The engineers have hairy ears*, my father used to sing.

\*

# V

# THE UNIVERSAL
# WIRE SERVICE

French is echoing on all sides. Excited voices, impatient voices, angry voices, lively voices.

*«Alors quoi[4]!»*

*«Mais dépêche-toi, nom de Dieu[5]...»*

*«Ah lalalalala!!»*

*«Eh, je fais ce que je peux[6]!»*

"Can you please proofread my story, Mr. Hertzen, please?"

"What's a good translation for *filibuster*?"

"Who's the new House Whip again?"

"How do you spell *anticonstitutionally*?"

All of a sudden, I am no longer in America. A little threshold, a door is all it takes. Zlumpka. Even the Americans who work here seem like outcasts or foreign. They are the ones who have to adapt.

I walk around the large newsroom with a wall of windows looking down on K Street, and wires spewing out copy on the other side, disgorging tons of paper, much of which will never be read but is there just in case. The reporters are not coming to the mountain so the mountain will come to them. I walk from messy to orderly desk, shaking hands with all my new colleagues or colleagues-to-be.

"Hey, how're you doing?" says Max-Hilaire Darquoix, the seldom-seen sports specialist. He is a short man whose absence of chin and fierce-looking though yellowish teeth recall an indistinct dog species, an impression reinforced by dull, seldom-washed hair.

---

4   -Well what??

5   -Well hurry for Christ's sake.

6   -Hey, I'm doing what I can!

I then go over to Hypolite Vazin. Although the Pentagon man, his gestures border on the delicate, not to say the effeminate, and his eyes bulge as though they have seen a lot, are traumatized by it, and are curious to see more.

Hubert Mascotte is the White House agent; while he is red in the face, as if he likes to hit the bottle, he has retained a certain innocence in his boyish good looks. Two men hold the business/finance desk: Nestor Petitcolis, a kind yet zesty grandfatherly type who likes to kid the girls — namely Clothilde Béarnaise who posed for Modigliani, long after the artist had died — and Félix Moutonneux, his tall, docile assistant, who would not be a bad looking fellow if he doubled his present weight.

And the "Desk" people: Pétard, Joffre, Douanel...

"Hello, Albert, how are you?" Hertzen the news director asks, placing a cigarette on the edge of an ashtray and looking down at it rather than at me. "Let me see what I've got for you today."

He is a medium height, middle-aged man with a strong chin and small eyes hidden behind horn-rimmed glasses. He shifts through his files and fishes up a large manila envelope which he informs me he has just received from the American Health Association.

"It seems as though they have found some kind of new way of measuring the growth of cholesterol in pregnant mothers; see what you can come up with. Keep it short, 200-250 words."

How would I feel in his shoes, I wonder? I look down on the grey carpeted floor for a second. For starters, my feet are a lot bigger; but, how does he decide where, how, why, when, what — the four *W*s and the *H* that compose the basis of the reversed pyramid which I and most other print media people have to figure out from one article to the next? How intimidating this all is at times. One has to assume it becomes second nature. First concentrate on the microcosm, the macro will follow. And then mackerel in white wine, which I have not tasted since I was at the Meaux high school but which I will savor one day again if I can show these people at UWS that I can fight like the rest. Pow! Pow! One-two, one-two! Diiiing! Though sometimes I am tired of fighting and would prefer to kick back and love.

I locate a vacant desk, swivel the swivel-chair around up and down till it reaches a height suitable to me, settle down behind a massive typewriter which types using a shiny, inky, massive font, pull the material out of the envelope, read it, analyze it, synthesize it, translate the quotes more literally than the rest, occasionally hanging on to my head lest I blow a fuse or two, and pound away. Tap-tap-tap-tap. The very sound of this mechanical Fred Astaire pushes me on. Tap-tap-tap-tap. Me, the former English major, appreciated by my photography professor, but always in conflict with the conveyors of literature. I'll show them a trick or two!

Tap-tap-tap-tap. Yes. I am getting into the swing of it, learning the new rhythm; this is a dispatch. How huge the letters! I walk over to Hertzen's office. He is on the telephone with Paris.

My God, Paris. The place still exists. Even though I no longer live there. Seems hard to believe. Even surrounded by all these émigrés. My family moved from Saint-Germain only three months ago, but it feels like three ice-ages. My memories are like dinosaurs inside a natural history museum. Impressive but held together by the pins, the nails, the rivets, the screws of memory.

Suddenly, there is a rap-a-tap-tap on the window pane separating Hertzen's office from the rest. There is Petitcolis, grandfatherly

Petitcolis, with a broad smile revealing many a precious metal, holding an issue of an American sports magazine displaying a particular beefy female body-builder. Hm, she looks a little like Anne Bradstreet, famous poet from Ipswich, Massachusetts and member of my graduating class.

When will I be at liberty to take such chances? I wonder under the folds of my reddish mustache. When will I show the boss my magazines? When will he think mine humorous? Ha! What if I had shown him that same magazine, rapping on this window in the same manner?

Hertzen has put down the phone. His jollity has waned. He adjusts his bifocals on a nose that could have inspired a social-realist artist — long but straight -, and starts to proofread the manuscript. Though slightly hidden by the strong chin, I can distinguish his red pen lashing forth, butchering my original prose. I close my eyes and clench my teeth.

"Not too bad," he concedes. "You have to learn to tighten your style. There are also a few spelling mistakes. Don't forget to always use sources; if you don't, the whole agency gets sued. We have a half-dozen cases pending as it is. Okay, type it up at one of the free consoles. And don't forget to add your initials at the bottom."

I write the name of the city, the date, UWS in parentheses, type a dash and on I go: *"A new device, enabling pregnant women to measure their cholesterol level has been successfully tested, the American Medical Association reports..."*

The green letters emerge like magic on the screen as my two indexes tap feverishly away, echoing the rhythm of dozens of other indexes around the room. Tic-tic-tic-tic. Except for Clothilde Béarnaise's who daintily uses ten fingers to type up the latest swings of the Stock Exchange. Some people are pigeon-toed, but the attractive henna-red head is pigeon-fingered; it is as though her hands are about to take flight any minute.

The lines of transmission are not too busy so I get to push the "send" button: blip, and voilà. *Le tour est joué.* Another story by Albert Nostran to be read around the world by millions of growing fans.

"You can take off if you want," Hertzen tells me as I stare at the presently empty screen.

Another hard day's work.

I walk back down K Street, headed for the Youth Hostel. The busiest artery in town is starting its daily human hemorrhage. Once again, I notice how 99 percent of the buildings are the same height and seem to have been erected between the 1950s and the present. Most are flat with a sea of desks, in and out trays, filing cabinets, electronic typewriters, bulletin boards, a few computers, and fluorescent lights, quite lifeless once you peer beyond the first floor reserved for retail. Steel and glass, as Lennon sings on the "Walls and Bridges" album.

Thank goodness for the Young Women's Christians Association. It is the right height for downtown: 12 stories, but the exterior red brick features crenellation, arches, fluting, a certain whimsy that the latter part of the century has chiseled away. Not efficient, as my college architecture professor would say. The big oak door gives. I walk inside. Find myself facing an ancient swerving royal staircase with alabaster columns leading up to the second floor. In the UWS building, as in most of the surrounding eyesores, there is just a stairwell hiding in shame behind steel doors, with exposed, sometimes not even painted cinder block — the same soulless cinder block that drove Ivan Denisovich mad in the gulag. The stairs are not a parenthesis, a safety measure, but an invitation, a way to move without having to be stationary in some sterile gymnasium. A way to see, an invitation to explore. Welcome, enter me, come and see my other floors. They are all very different, titillatingly irregular.

My legs say gladly. I have penetrated a vast dark room. The venetian blinds have been pulled. A streak of white is all the light available. Secrets linger here, mysteries. No longer do I tread the land of the obvious and the commonplace. I feel I am walking through a dream designed by Salvador Dalí and Luis Buñuel. At the end of this room, in the far left corner stands an upright piano. O miracle of miracles, the keyboard is not even locked. I lift the cover, keys await. I play a few notes, my fingers warm up, get excited, itchy, begin to canter like horses in a cropped hayfield.

"ARE YOU A MEMBER?" A voice grunts.

A little black man walks towards me.

"No."

"YOU CAN'T PLAY THAT PIANO."

"Sorry."

Grunt.

I return down the majestic stairway to the oak door to the street. Too bad there is not an apartment house to inject a little life in these quarters. But this is not Central Park West and there is no Dakota in sight.

Darkness is descending, the office crowd has retired down the freeway and through rail-lined tunnels to the grassy outskirts, and new creatures appear on the sidewalk. Women. Slow-moving women with short skirts and low-cut blouses. Bottoms that sway, breasts pressed together, trying to look larger than they really are. If you could squeeze their eyes like a lemon, amazing stories would trickle out.

They meander around K and L between 14th and 15th, emerging from the stripped-down background, from the cracks, like dandelions in the sidewalk. Prostitution, a form of death in its denial of love, in the ephemeral twinkle of pleasure it claims to produce, injects this part of the city with a certain life. Like in the alleys of the Bois de Boulogne, by the Pré Catlan, cars and pickup — o zesty double-entendre! — trucks slow down. The black, white, sometimes oriental ladies emerge from behind pillars and doorways and strut towards the lined-up vehicles: "Do you want a date?" they ask. What a farce! And yet, how romantic, in the Baudelairian sense. This is Monet territory no longer. They pry open the doors of perspiring men's cars, making it hard for the driver to expel them.

"How much?" the men ask.

"Fifty."

As I near my transitory abode I spot the flashing signs on 14th Street. "This Is It," announces one of them, while across the street, another cluster of patient ladies await behind a two-way mirror storefront above which one can read "Massage Parlor." I do not feel too much stress so I think I shall avoid the place for now. I am more in the mood for a good book and a good meal. Perhaps something Californian. Down the street I spot a Ronald Reagan's.

*

# VI

# CRAZY THINGS

"How do you do, Albert? Shall we have lunch today?" Dominique Mouluvert, the big, bald boss suggests, rather coincidentally, given the end of the last chapter, and, since I was beginning to get hungry anyhow.

"Sure."

Sounds good to me, Mr. Bald Boss.

I follow the tall, athletic, bald figure out the glass door of the K Street building. Somehow, I am reminded of a German World War II general. Below his shiny dome he is wearing an expensive-looking dark-brown three-piece suit and seems to be aware of his allure even though he would get a failing grade as far as his nose goes. It does not quite possess Hertzen's art deco allure. Or mine. Although my eyes are small and slanted — "pig's eyes," a woman once informed me — my nose would do any Roman, friend or countryman proud. Still, I admire the fashion in which the prince of the Universal Press Wire struts across the streets as through his personal domain.

Like in New York, the gridiron pattern, contrary to what some foreigners may assume, does not spell sterility. Not at this time of day. Cars honk, people yell; from bureaucrats to painters, from lawyers to building engineers, from office managers to secretaries. Composers jot down notes and tear their partition up because they are dissatisfied. Stone Harbor, I miss thee not.

Mouluvert has led me into a brasserie. The smell of fresh baked bread fills the air and blends with the scent of herbs and coffee. Sunlight splashes gaily through the room. This is the life. He seems to know the manager, a ruddy-faced, blonde French woman. He orders a *choucroute garnie*. Lost in the menu's choices and intimidated by some of the pricier items, I feel safe ordering the same thing.

"By the way, who told you about the agency?" Baldy interrogates.

I tell him about Bridget, the waitress at the Marinader Inn married to a Frenchman who, while job-searching for her husband, lent me a helping hand; how because of my languages I was led to translation.

"But you must remember that you are not a translator now. The people who work at UWS are journalists who translate; there is a big difference," he says with a slight sneer in his voice and in his left nostril. His eyes remind me of an elephant's. Something about the dark eyelid.

"Certainly. Actually, my own father was a journalist."

"Oh? For what organization?"

"He mostly worked for Thyme."

"You use the past tense..."

"He has retired."

"I might have met him when I worked in Paris; what's his name?"

"Quentin Nostran."

"Hm. Quentin Nostran. No, I'm afraid it doesn't ring a bell."

How can anyone not have heard of Quentin Nostran? The young reporter that Dino Grandi called upon during the last days of Mussolini! The war correspondent who took a pee in the Battle of the Bulge alongside Patton and Churchill! Then ripped off a Nazi flag from a Belgian town hall... and whose poem on the Second World War appeared on the front page of the New York Times the day the Germans surrendered! The bard who showed an approving Ezra Pound his poetry! The bohemian who lived above John Dos Passos in Greenwich Village! The music lover who, during a party on Long Island, sat next to Gershwin while the latter was hammering away at the keyboard! The pugilist who got into a fist fight with Clark Gable! The journalist who (in the company of his beautiful wife) interviewed Salvador Dalí (in Figueras), Joan Miró (Minorca), Calder (somewhere in France), Chagall (Provence), Red Adair (Algeria), Richard Addams (Isle of Man), Herbert von Karajan (Paris); downed whiskey with Faulkner; dined at the same table as Kennedy and De Gaulle (of whom he was not the greatest fan); attended Josephine Baker's funeral. The writer whose article on Jules Verne has become a modern classic... *"Sit down Monsieur; you must be exhausted after all this traveling!"* The art aficionado and painter whose articles embraced not only the living but El Greco, Rembrandt, Caravaggio, Rubens, Titian, Bosch, Hogarth, Turner, Goya, Delacroix, Gauguin, Utrillo, Vlaminck, Escher... AND THIS DOES NOT RING A BELL? Life goes on beyond the Universal Press Wire!

The blonde waitress brings two steaming plates to the table.

"Be careful," she warns, "it's hot."

"We'll make a note of that," says Mouluvert, the gentleman. To me: "So how does it feel to be entering the career of journalism?"

"I'm enjoying it a lot. I love the nature of the work, to be writing, reporting, to be aware of the last changes as they are happening. Too bad my compatriots are such an apathetic lot when it comes to the rest of the world."

"Well, Albert, you know, America is a big country. There is so much to cover from coast to coast. It's normal that people are interested about what is happening in their own back garden."

"Still, sometimes it seems that people overseas are better informed about America than its own inhabitants."

"It's true that there is tendency here to focus on different matters. I remember when I used to take the bus in the morning and the average fellow would hold on to the sports and business section and throw the rest of the paper away without having read the headlines."

"They did?"

"Like I'm telling you. Come on and eat, don't wait for me."

Getting bolder, while adding a hint of mustard to spice up the sausage, I express my lack of enthusiasm for a lot of the surrounding architecture.

"I sort of like it myself," retorts Mouluvert. "It's clean, rational, functional. When I first got here in the late 50s, there were a bunch of Victorian row houses. Something you'd imagine in Georgetown or around Logan Circle. Shepherd's Row, I think it was called. Can't say I was sad to see them go."

Victorian row houses? God, it must have been so grand! How could they have demolished them? That's what Pop must have known when he lived down here as a young man, shortly before the tail-fin/zoot suit era. Always the nebulous one, Pop never did talk much about those days. I am sure Anne Bradstreet, the poet from Ipswich, Burdon graduate and femme fatale body-builder extraordinaire, would have seconded my opinion. She understood. Ah, Anne! We hardly knew thee before looking up Ipswich in the *Encyclopedia Britannica* and still do not know much. The question is: did she know of Emily Dickinson, though the latter was her junior by roughly a century?

"So you grew up in France?" Mouluvert asks. "You do speak the language without the trace of an accent. That's exactly like my daughters, except in reverse. They were raised in India, England and the States, although they did attend French schools and passed their *baccalauréat*[7]."

"I passed mine in Meaux."

And am enjoying the sauerkraut and sausages. It beats Ronald Reagan's any day.

"Meaux? Meaux? That's fairly close to Paris, isn't it?"

"About 40 kilometers east, when you're heading towards Chalons-sur-Marne and the Champagne region. It's famous for its Brie cheese, its grainy mustard — Pomery — and its gothic cathedral."

---

7  -The exam one takes at the end of French secondary school.

Michael Kent

"That's where Archbishop Bossuet wrote his famous eulogies, I believe."

"Exactly."

Finally, someone on the American continent who can place Meaux — and not ask whether it is anywhere near "Ho," like one Neanderthal (low forehead, very short chin, broom-like hair, rich daddy) uttered one cloudy evening at Burdon. After his girlfriend had remarked that I was "one of those empty-plate people." That, folks, is *Hyar Edukashun*.

"You know," Moulu says, as his knife is prying one of the sausages open, if you prove to be a good worker, this job could lead you around the world. Think of it. I started off myself in Morocco, spent time in Burma. That's where my second daughter was born."

"Is that right?"

Both our plates are empty, the check arrives, Mouluvert hands over a wad of cash, and it's time to go back to work.

I am about to complete my second draft an hour later — about a string of women demonstrating around the Pentagon — when my gaze gets distracted by Mouluvert, seated behind one of the VDTs, rather than in the seclusion of his office. Like some of the other *agenciers*, he types with two fingers. But, while I keep my wrist in alignment with my forearm and the lower part of my hand parallel to the desk and to the keyboard, Moulu's wrists are bent and his hands are perpendicular like a hawk about to pounce on a mouse, and his indexes look as though they were trying to emulate the legs of a flamenco dancer. He looks at them as though in a narcissistic trance. How much faster than a policeman filling out a form! My father also types with two fingers but never looks at them. Of course, there tends to be a certain number of words containing excessive amounts of Zs and Xs.

Before I have time to digress any further, big bald boss calls me over to his terminal and asks me to proofread his latest master work. It is an editorial, in English, about the United States flexing its industrial muscle, starting with a quote from Chrysler Chairman Lee Iacocca: "America is not going to get pushed around anymore." Go Chrysler, go! The style is good, perhaps a little British, but more power to it. I nod approvingly.

"Very good Albert," he says in English. "Thank you very much."

I return to the Youth Hostel quite elated. And in record time.

\*    \*    \*

My God, he made it. Not only does the most popular fast food chain in the District of Columbia bear his name but he has actually made it to the presidency. Ex-California Governor Ronald Reagan, the "drugstore truck-driving man," as they called him at Woodstock, the gas-station attendant, as one cartoonist nailed him down to, has become our 40th president. I feel as though I have been clobbered over the head by an anvil with enough rubber around it to soften the blow but not deaden the impact completely. When this man fights he wears the gloves. Jimmy Carter talked about the American malaise. Wrong move, Mr. Peanut Farmer. You do not tell the American folk that they are erring, as true as that as that may be.

Doctor Reagan has comes along with his magic wand and carpet bag and said that all is fine. Cut taxes, rules and regulations, slash into big government while arming up. The marketplace will take care of it all. Sort of like telling a patient: "You don't have a cancerous tumor. Just take a shot of Mylanta." So the untreated problem festers and spreads. Pretty soon the patient is dead.

On the chair next to mine there is a Norwegian fellow watching the news on the television set in the Youth Hostel's lounge.

"Don't the Americans have any sense? It's appalling to elect such an individual."

"I'll say. Do you want to get a beer down the street?" I suggest.

"Yeah. Let's drown the pain."

At the bar down the street, there is a small group of men and women dressed to the nines, three-piece suits, silk dresses, roaring with delight. Champagne corks are popping. Part of the Californian concoction ends up on the rug. They start to sing. Trying to fill the void of the night, it seems, trying to convince themselves that there is no void and that there is no night.

"America has gone insane," the Norwegian guy says looking at the group in disbelief.

"Let's go to a less cheerful place," I suggest.

"Good idea."

\*    \*    \*

Michael Kent

The following morning in the foyer as I am peering out at the park across the street I meet a fellow, an American this time, who, judging by his conversation on the payphone is also looking for more permanent living quarters.

"You want a place near the Metro," he explains to me after hanging up the receiver. "Because in this town, if you don't have a car, it's the only decent means to get around. A good place to look, by the way, if you don't mind sharing, is the George Washington University housing agency."

We both walk over to the Student Center seven blocks away, passing for G.W.U. students. A couple of plump ladies smile at us. I jot down a couple of numbers. The first two people I attempt to contact turn out to be gay and have no desire to share their premises with a heterosexual; the third asks me if I have adopted the alternative lifestyle.

"No," I answer. "I like women."

"That's good. You have no idea the number of gay guys who call. They get especially excited when I tell them I'm a tennis pro."

"I bet."

"Do you smoke?"

"No."

"Where are you from?"

"Massachusetts."

"Oh really? One of my best friends is from the Boston area. How about that? I'm from New Jersey myself. You say you're just out of college?"

"Yes."

"So am I. That's a pretty neat coincidence, isn't it?"

"Yeah."

I find it hard to put my whole heart into such neat coincidences.

"Are you employed?"

"Yes. I work at the Universal Wire Service."

"Never heard of it, but it sounds impressive. I'm trying to get into TV journalism myself. In the meantime I work at a Ronald Reagan's."

"Give it time."

"You're not Jewish, are you?"

"No."

"You're not? That's too bad. Of course, I am. That would have been really perfect if you had been, because it seems like we have a lot in common. You know, your voice sounds almost exactly like my best friend's who's from Boston. Another coincidence. I would have thought... Well, do you want to come over and see the place?"

"Sure."

"Like the ad says, it's a duplex with a nice large living room and you'd have your own individual room. Naturally, we'd have to share a bathroom; I hope you don't mind that?"

"That's fine by me. When may I come over?"

"Er... How about later on today? Do you drive?"

"Yes, but I don't have a car."

So, like in the movies, rather than explaining something twice, I am already taking the Metro, enjoying its high futuristic yet somehow Raphaelite vaults, from McPherson Square, the station I equate with Pigalle and sin, to the Pentagon, which I must confess is a great disappointment. No wonder they always shoot, so to speak, the building from the air, because from the ground it is a mass of sinister, desolate grey concrete around which hundreds of buses await to carry the passengers to various Northern Virginian suburbs. It seems all the buses in the world are fuming there, except the one leading to Mapletree Park. I should have brought along a book to read. Ten minutes later however, my bus shows up, leading me away from this nut of an edifice past Highway 395 to Sycamore Lane. Sycamore Lane, where Davey Gronket awaits.

Michael Kent

There is a bit of a breeze. I walk up the street. Long red-brick buildings with white neo-colonial doorframes, with a Chippendale crown, stand on either side. There is a certain stillness in the air and dead leaves strew the ground. The sky is skim-milk white. I am carried back to college. Autumn is the college season.

I look to the left. 4139, 4141. There it is. I ring the doorbell. A fellow in his early twenties with a hairstyle reminiscent of the early Beatle days and a smile displaying slightly imperfect teeth opens the door.

"Hi! You must be Albert; I'm Davey, Davey Gronket. Welcome."

Hello Davey, Davey Gronket.

I find the enthusiasm pleasant, though I am personally incapable of responding in such a manner. Simon, my brother, has accused me of being snobbish, but actually I am just a little reserved when I do not know someone very well. Besides, one has to draw the line somewhere.

We climb up a first blonde wooden staircase which leads up to the dining room. It boasts a couple of easy chairs, a bean bag, and a small brown-plaid sofa. My favorite color, if I were to be insincere. A Chrysler air-conditioner is wedged into the back wall.

"There's the TV. It used to have a full-color spectrum but now it only seems to play green. Personally, I don't mind it. Come this way; let me show you the kitchen. It has every modern convenience you can think of: a spacious refrigerator, plenty of storage space, a dishwasher, an *insinkerator*."

He points out a switch above the stainless steel sink. Something about that word *"insinkerator"* forces me to wince. It seems so unnatural, a certain epitome of practicality, of Americanness gone awry. I almost feel nauseous.

"So, what do you think so far?"

"It's pretty nice."

"Wait 'till I show you the upstairs!"

I can't wait.

He has acquired the far bigger room, which includes an impressive stack of 1960s Playboy magazines and tennis equipment strewn around the floor. Yet the smaller room also boasts a large window with a perfect view of the next building which has been erected parallel to this one and hides Highway 395. The bathroom's bathtub strikes me as a little grayish on the bottom but that is nothing that cannot be fixed.

"Is the Pentagon the nearest subway stop?"

"For the moment, but they're planning a nearer one in a few years."

Both of us will probably be dead by that time, but let us not quibble about minor details.

"How much are you asking again?"

"Well, I'm not the one asking — it's the rental company, but the price is $220 a month."

Hm, that's quite reasonable. Davey seems a decent chap, easy to get along with, even though I am personally not the greatest tennis player that ever walked the face of the earth. Besides, I am not going to spend the rest of my life here or precious time looking for a better deal.

"I think I'm interested," I say.

"Great! I still have a couple of people to see before I decide who's going to be moving in, but I'll say you stand an excellent chance."

"Good. I'm now staying at the youth hostel downtown, and it's sort of difficult to reach me, so why don't I give you a call tomorrow?"

"Later on tonight will be fine."

"Okay."

And later that night we did indeed wrap up this minor detail.

"I'm really looking forward to living with you," he says, "you seem like a very nice guy."

I smiled the smile of skulls, amused at this Davey Gronket's perpetual buoyancy, but was actually not dreading the thought of leaving this transient area where the semen of perverts clings to the air.

Not too sure as to where to go for a bite to eat, I ended up enjoying the salad bar. At Ronald Reagan's, or, as we say in French: *chez* Ronald Reagan. *Chez Monsieur le gouverneur de Californie.* Perhaps he will make a good president; he does have an impressive head of hair.

\*

# VII

# FAILING TO SEE THE LOGIC

"I don't have a bed," I tell Davey, staring down at the naked parquet floor. There is a slight echo when I talk.

"That's right, you don't. Let's look in the local paper; they often have good deals there."

Gronket has a solution for everything.

"I'll say."

We browse. The pages crumple. The sun has set, little lights twinkle twankle twonkle in the Northern Virginian inkiness.

"Wasn't that a good game last night?" he stipulates.

"A fine game it was. Until the very end it was hard to see who had really won."

"Oh, here's one that's not too far away."

"Oh good."

Davey dials the phone number; although he does not know the people from Adam, he seems to be having a merry old conversation, giggling and joking away, the way Americans are prone to do at any time of the day or night. I would not move from this country for all the mangos in China.

We hop into his Pinto.

"Believe or not," he tells me, "I really like this car."

"Isn't this the one that explodes when you rear end it?"

He stares at the road, probably because he is a prudent driver.

"Originally yes, but Ford has fixed the problem for free. It has a certain sporty quality that you don't find in some of the bigger models."

"The gauges are designed in an attractive way."

"Yeah, real sporty."

He rips around the corners; the shocks make a clanky sound. My knees are at about ear level. How my new apartment-mate can find his way around all these remarkably identical-looking streets is beyond me. To him, they seem pleasant, filled with happy homes with jolly Americans. I attempt to identify. One day I will, one day I will. I feel a slight rumble in my stomach.

"Okay, this is it."

Like the strip joint on 14th Street.

We slam the heavy doors shut which are almost in perfect alignment with the rest of the vehicle. Watch out world, here come Nostran and Gronket. Batman Nostran and his groovy chauffeur Robin Gronket, famous adventurers one day, suave newscasters the next.

"Well, hellooo," a woman with a nose not unlike Karl Malden's or a little potato, short black hair, and an engaging smile opens the door to greet us. "We're all watchin' Dallas and we don't know if J.R. is gonna make it."

Jesus Christ woman, pull yourself together!

"I say he pulls through!" the energetic, not easily undaunted Davey responds.

We enter the cozy apartment. Our feet and soon our ankles sink into wall-to-wall tan carpeting with more bounce to it than the average trampoline. Our eyes are arrested by furniture that bears antique shape but is sparkling new. Perhaps this is a condominium and all hell will break loose.

"Y'all wanna grab a seat?" a boyfriend asks, eyes glued to the big color screen framed by a case resembling the Parthenon. He sports long mutton-chop sideburns and his brown hair is greased back à la Roy Orbison and shows hardly any trace of dandruff. Polyester yellow is a good color for that.

I thought we were in Northern Virginia but it now seems we have landed in Southern Georgia.

Images drift by on the tube full of people with expensive clothes and glittering smiles, but I cannot seem to make heads or tails of it whereas the three others are visibly in a trance. What is wrong with me? I ask the good Lord.

"Well," the boyfriend says during a commercial break, "I guess y'all wanted to take a peek at the mattress and box-springs, as I was tellin', er, Davey here over the phone. It's in real good condition. You do like a hard mattress, don't you?"

"Wouldn't want any other kind," I say.

"Yeah. I think you're gonna like this one. I guess we'd better get movin'. Okay Eleonore, I'll be seein' you in a bit."

"Y'all take care; see you later Abe," says Eleonore as we bounce on the rug and reach the door. She does not have Ivory girl skin but her navy-blue sweater becomes her.

We follow Abe in the Pinto through a new maze of streets down to a larger apartment building complex. Once again, I notice Davey's unflappable faith in the residential environment that seems to go on ad infinitum, interrupted now and again by the local chain of convenience stores whose soapy odor permeates the nose forever.

Glass doors, lobby, security man, elevator, long hall, key in the lock, knob turns.

"Excuse the mess, fellows. This is it back in this corner."

I look the mattress over.

"Yeah, it's got a couple of stains, don't know how they got there but they're real old anyhow. Nothing a clean set of sheets won't cover up."

"May I test drive it?" I ask.

"Here are the keys." We all laugh heartily.

I lie down. It is firm but comfortable; no spring is attacking my rib cage. I hardly feel like getting up again.

"How much are you asking for it?"

"Well it's still in pretty good condition... I was thinking around $100.

"A hundred? How about 50?" I suggest.

He scratches the back of his head while his black-rimmed glasses look down at the mattress.

"Oh, what the heck. I just want to get rid of it really."

"How about that marble table in the corner?"

"Oh, I almost forgot about that one. Well, yeah, it's for sale too. I'll let you have it for twenty dollars."

"Fifteen."

"Okay."

We return downstairs, load the mattress up on the roof of the Pinto, fold the back seat to accommodate the table, and drive back to Mapletree Park, happy as nightingales.

"I'll lend you some sheets until you get your own," Davey says with a grin which for some reason reminds me of a gibbon's.

*   *   *

"There're no curtains or blinds on the windows," I tell Davey on my first night in the new abode.

"So what? I don't need them. You'll get used to it."

I look out at the night salted with fluorescent dots and mercury vapor fumes.

*     *     *

Washington, city of museums. Back in the Burdon days, my roommate Jake used to rave about the Hirshhorn. So I took the subway to the Smithsonian Station and decided I would investigate matters for myself. There, after the Freer Gallery and the brick castle, it stood: a concrete doughnut. I rode the escalator up to the second floor. The good thing about museums is not only the static statues but also the mobile ones.

Near me are two charming lasses, a tall brunette and a shorter redhead with a funny turned up nose and a ponytail. Our paths seem to run parallel. My, that brunette is something, a doe turned human. From bust to bust, this little game goes on. Ah, there he is: Baudelaire. I stop and concentrate on the man who opened the doors of literature and poetry to me.

"It's quite a work, isn't it? Rodin has a most powerful style."

I look around. My God, the redhead. She is there a couple of feet away from me. Perhaps not my first choice but the brunette has obviously another cud on which to chew. I look more closely. Her green smock reveals frontal assets that rule out much of the competition. How kind and inviting. And though her nose turns upward and her ears do stick out a trifle, her face is actually quite pretty, particularly when she smiles. Good Celtic stock.

"I sort of like it myself. It's nice to get away from all that abstract stuff. So much of the twentieth century is a wasteland. It seems to have picked up momentum after the Second World War."

My response, as unimpressive as it sounds, appears to be generating a longer conversation.

"I agree." She laughs approvingly. Her brown eyes stare at me intently.

"I'm going upstairs," the taller woman said.

"See you in a bit, Ann."

All of the Night

Like me, Jillian has studied English and art and has recently graduated from some little college down in Virginia somewhere. She giggles a lot as I make silly comments about a row of most somber-looking statues.

"Do you live in Washington?" she asks.

"Actually, in Park Mapletree, Virginia, but it's not very far from here."

"Oh? That must be nice. I live in Richmond with my parents."

Too far but it's worth asking her for her address.

"Maybe we can get together again sometime," I suggest.

"Oh yes, that would be fun. Oh by the way, this is my friend Ann."

The timid doe has reemerged. She looks at me with less suspicion than before. The three of us leave the museum walking down the Mall towards the Washington Monument. We part in front of the Metro station as the sky turns a pale yellow and the earth dons the black cloak of evening. What a city this is. But Richmond? Tsk. So very impractical.

*    *    *

I walk and I walk and I walk and I keep on walking. I do not exercise much, but I can walk on until the soles of my shoes wear out. Down Constitution Avenue, past more museums, vast expanses of rolling grass, into the sunset, feeling like a poor lonesome dude and a long way from home. Up Virginia Avenue, past the State Department monolith, a gloomy complex that would have made Joseph Stalin feel perfectly cuddly, and the Pan American Health Organization, that funny 1960s beehive fantasy. ANYONE HOOOOOOME? No, for nobody lives here. No one was intended to live here. This is the land of the post-apocalypse.

I am the sole survivor. In a sense, it is nice to enjoy the broad avenues of Bureaucratland by myself. I cross a couple of highways and I reach the John Fitzgerald Kennedy Center for the Performing Arts. The fortress in the middle of traffic. Where the Olde Heurich Brewery used to process lager yeast, Cascade hops, and caramel malt[8]. I enter under the highest ceilings I think I have ever seen. A feeling

8    -"To reach a frothy head," quotes the bottle's label since the beer was resuscitated (although brewed in Utica, N.Y.) in the late 1980s.

of peace looms. Tranquility. Serenity. To the right is the American Film Institute. They are playing Rainer Werner Fassbinder's "Mother Küsters Goes to Heaven." Fassbinder. The name rings a definite bell. I like the title. Am I smiling outwardly or just inside? A movie is a movie. I can think of worse places. I buy a ticket, and go to heaven too.

\* \* \*

A chalky morning. Just missed the bus to the Pentagon, so I will hitchhike. The day is overcast and after a couple of minutes a Gremlin stops. A Gremlin! Those cars with the sawed-off diagonal back have always intrigued me; they are both odd and quintessentially American. A silvery-blonde fleece awaits inside. With a smile included free of charge.

"I'm going to Union Station," she says.

I must be a fine-looking or at least respectable-looking young man for such a lovely woman to give me a lift.

"Perfect," I say, trying not to notice too overtly her many charms. On what Ukrainian plain have we met before? We putter down I-395. The freeway strikes me as more beautiful than it ever has in the bus dieseling its way to the Pentagon.

"You know, I never pick anyone up," she mentions, staring with her light blue eyes at the road ahead. "So you grew up in France?" she adds, as the conversation purrs along. "I spent my junior year abroad in Nancy."

"Nancy has a nice railroad station as I recall."

"A lot of other nice things too."

She swings a right on Constitution, past the Mall that Pierre L'Enfant intended as a Washingtonian Champs Elysées but is now a grassy field.

"Did you like it?"

"Yes. I think it would have been a shame to have concrete."

"No, I mean Nancy."

"Oh, I loved it; they have these old buildings, a beautiful 18th century square... *La Place Stanislas* — is that how you pronounce it? But I never get the opportunity to speak the language anymore. Oh, it looks like we're arriving. By the way, my name is Deborah.

Listen, let me give you my phone number and you can stop by some time. You live in Park Mapletree, don't you?"

"Just moved in."

"Okay, bye."

La-la-la-la-la. I look back at the phone number and address. And off that funny looking little car zooms in the misty dawn while I head towards the Metro to catch the red line to Farragut North where another exciting day at the job awaits. I peer up at the station's tall venerable vaults, clutch a white column as I walk on. There has been talk of tearing it down. NO! NO!

*　　*　　*

Davey, after taking off his plastic cowboy hat and his bright red nylon shirt, has prepared dinner for me — Chicken Khachaturian — to feast his new apartment-mate. Khachaturian, and you're sitting on top of the world. I thought I would buy a bottle of rosé for the occasion.

"Usually, I don't drink," he says. No perhaps it is around the eyes that he looks most monkey-like. They are beady and shrewd. A man who does not drink. I get suspicious.

"Come on, this is a festive occasion."

"Okay, but just a little bit."

I remember my father's contempt for people who used to come to the house and when offered spirits used to say: "*just a little bit.*"

"To our friendship," he says, lifting his glass.

To our friendship? What is this? I feel as though I am imprisoned in some bad TV commercial. Perhaps I have inherited my father's superstition but such a toast seems forced and begging for trouble. Perhaps it is the Chinese in me. Or the mangos.

Our glasses cling. A few minutes later I pour myself another while Davey's remains depressingly full.

"The chicken's good," I tell him.

"Yeah; I consider myself a pretty good cook."

"I'm worthless in the kitchen."

"You'll learn."

At the end of the meal, the wine level in his glass has not budged. Hm. perhaps a centimeter. I do not blame him entirely, it is rather sweet. Still.

"I'll do the dishes," I offer.

"Okay, be sure to scrub them well. Like I said, I'm a bit of a Felix Unger when it comes to neatness," he responds, referring to "The Odd Couple" TV show. "I'm going to watch a little TV. *Dallas* is coming on."

Count me out.

I walk up to my room and write an ode to Deborah and her funny looking car. She should get it in tomorrow's mail. I look up at the ceiling and decide to give her a ring.

"Oh, Albert, I'm so glad you called. Do you want to come over for a drink next Friday? That way you can meet my two roommates."

Roommates?

"I'd be delighted."

La-la-la-la.

*   *   *

Friday has come and gone. I flip on the television set to be sermoned about the evils of bad breath. Sometimes it seems as the whole philosophy of the United States pivots around unpleasant odors. George Washington started the long tradition with his rotten wooden dentures. Warren Harding, a lover of Mexican cuisine, suffered from gas, although this is more speculative. Friday has come and gone.

Then they played *"Casablanca."* The green version, that is, on Davey's TV set while he was serving burgers, fries, and tooth-melters at the Ronald Reagan's at the nearby shopping center. Nearby meaning if you have a car. My, what a film. I think I started to lose it when the airplane's second propeller begins to rotate. I felt funny around the throat, I think my eyes started to get moist. Has there ever been an actress more beautiful than Ingrid Bergman? But Rick let her go.

Friday has come and gone and I am hung over from the gin and tonics I had down the street at Deborah's. Her roommates had taken off. This favored my darkest schemes.

"I received your poem," she said. "I thought it was pretty good. I was reminded a little of Byron."

*Hail muses, etc.*

"Thank you."

"Have a seat."

I sat on the couch.

She walked over to the stereo and placed Schumann's Third Symphony on the turntable only to return to an armchair. Hey, there's room on the couch!

"I love the romantics," she said, "Blake, Keats, Shelley... The whole lot."

The armchair complicated my plans. Why did she not join me on the couch? This was a bad sign.

"Did you ever study Baudelaire?"

"Yeah; I remember reading a couple of his poems back in the Nancy days. Pretty bleak stuff as I recall. Oh, what's the time? I think "Dallas" is about to start."

From Byron to Baudelaire to "Dallas" in one fell swoop. They say one has to adapt to the times, but I found it difficult to sit through one whole episode and announced that I was going to retire. She would have to get up to say goodbye. This would enable me to implement plan 14-B. I thought the opportunity ripe. It was either too ripe or not ripe enough because, as my lips were about to indulge in the most natural of all acts, she turned her head away, and all I could feel was a cheekbone.

"I don't think so," she said. The tone was so innocent yet cutting I rushed to the toilet and vomited.

"That's the problem, you shouldn't think," I said coming back after a swig of Listerine. No wonder mouthwash is so popular in this country.

"Let's not rush into anything, okay?"

"Fine."

I took off up the hill in the night. It was probably a mistake to slam the door and call her a cock-teaser. Thank God I have the job. O dear precious job. Because my social life is like a, er, like a threadbare rug or overcoat, not keeping me too warm. And definitely no bounce. Why can a man and a woman not copulate without this complex ritual, all these little games?

Perhaps I should grow my beard back; women seem more attracted to me when I have a beard. A mustache alone doesn't quite cut it. You just look like an overly suave guy in a cigarette commercial.

Simon, my brother in Syracuse, corroborates the matter over the phone.

"You'll never believe what this one chick told me at a party I went to the night of the elections." His voice is quite deep. He smokes and I do not.

"Night of the living dead," I add sympathetically.

"Precisely. That since he was elected president, Ronald Reagan is the best American."

"The best American. What the hell does that mean? I fail to see the logic."

"Man, I don't know what Washington is like, but this place is the pits. Not particularly beautiful, a lot of the students are these little rich kids from Long Island; totally obsessed with cars, clothes, material status. I'm not used to that shit. At least when you went to college you had France to look forward to. Me, I've got Stone Harbor, Massachusetts. What is Stone Harbor to me? I don't have friends there or memories. I feel this sense of emptiness."

"But at least you can drive back there, call the folks up. Speaking of which, I hope Mum's okay. Pop's still not talking to me."

"Yeah. Strangely enough he's been pretty nice to me and actually to Mum."

"That's some good news. I hope things get better for you and I'll call you in a week or so."

"Thanks. *Ciao, bambino.*"

"*Ciao, ragazzo.*"

*   *   *

Davey did try. I suppose I should give him that. Last night we drove off in his baby-blue Pinto towards the District.

"Wow, this is beautiful!" I exclaimed as the car plodded over Memorial Bridge.

There was the Lincoln Memorial all lit up, pillars emerging against a golden glow, its grandeur burning in the night.

"Isn't it though? This is some city!"

"I'll say."

"Rachel is a bit of a pain in the butt but she throws pretty good parties."

We parked on M Street, N.W. in the West End and walked over to the handsome row-house where Rachel, a friend of Davey's lives. She had invited a large number of people over that night. Meandering through bodies and noise, I attempted to strike up a conversation with some of the guests, one with a fat Irish type who works in the White House.

"And what do you do?" he asks.

"I work at the Universal Wire Service."

"Oh, that sounds fairly interesting."

Why the "fairly?" The way he insisted on the word. Screw him. *Scroom all,* as Pop would say. The old man and I have a lot in common; why don't we get along?

I walked around the bustling room, digging into the hors d'oeuvres. Rachel herself was the quintessentially bubbly hostess, prone to screaming with delight now and then as she recognized a familiar or it seems even an unfamiliar face. Somehow all the talk started to blend into one big cacophony, so I settled in an armchair and pulled out *Dracula*, the original, by Bram Stoker.

"You're okay Albert?" Rachel asks, leaning towards me.

"Oh, I'm fine."

Just let me read.

Actually, Rachel herself appears quite friendly and not unattractive. I like the way she cuts her hair in a sort of 1920s style. The mistake was to go to the party. I am still brooding over the Deborah fiasco. Such a pleasant smile though. Rachel's or anyone else's in the room does not come anywhere near it. Coca Cola compared to Lambrusco. Fried chicken compared to coq-au-vin.

"Why did you have to read in front of all my friends?" Davey asked me in a nasal, disagreeable tone of voice on the way back to Park Mapletree.

"I didn't feel I had too much in common with any of the people there."

"But do you realize what it looks like to start reading a book in the middle of a party?"

"I suppose."

A mile goes by.

"The first guy you started talking to can organize a special tour of the White House. Go beyond the usual tourist thing."

"That would be interesting."

And he is such a jolly good fellow. *Fairly* interesting. I swear.

\*

# VIII

# THE GRAVEYARD SHIFT

M id-November. It had to happen and it did: the graveyard shift. Midnight to nine a.m. After two and a half weeks of mostly sun. This is after all why I was plucked from my non-native Massachusetts. *To replace a man who was losing his sanity.*

I have taken the bus back to the Pentagon and the subway to Farragut West, walked down vacated Farragut Square down to K Street. K for kwiet. K for kalm. Mimi, the secretary with the sunken black eyes and the aquiline nose, has given me my predecessor's magnetic card to enter the building after hours. A strange expression when you think of it. "After hours." There are the hours per se and then the vacuum, the vacuum of the night.

The newsroom is empty except for Achilles Pétard, one of the generalists, who one week a month has to assume the pre-graveyard shift. I had been struck from the beginning by the jet-black hair he wore down to his shoulders, trying to imagine such a sight in an American office, though his is not so much like a hippie's rather than a soldier's in the Napoleonic guard or a minister of Louis XIV, accentuating a pale face slit sideways by lips thin enough to cut through glass. Although his erect posture and general manner might lead one to think that he is hiding the fact that he has just lost or won a bullfight, he is the one always exchanging jokes with Mimi and Dido, the two secretaries, only to break out now and then in a manic, bone-chilling laughter. He has been assigned tonight to guide me through the routine, but tomorrow I will be left to myself to survey the Associated Press wire and catch the news-breaking stories.

"Don't hesitate to call me or Mr. Mouluvert," Hertzen had urged the day before as the afternoon light was still beaming in through the windows. "Here are all the numbers."

He pointed out the list of all the newsroom personnel typed on a sheet of paper tacked to one of the columns. Including the accountant, Ambroise Tartignole. My name was not on that list. Not on that list *yet*. Most of the people lived in Maryland, some in Virginia, a minority resided in the District, something that struck me as difficult to understand. UWS accountant Tartignole has suggested I live in Virginia for tax purposes; is there life beyond taxes?

"First thing," says Pétard, "is to always read the board; see what others have covered during the day to avoid repeats and keep abreast of what's going on. So you also have to study the international board. It shows the wire's entire production over the last 24 hours or so. It's a lot to read, but you have to, it's the nature of the job. If an emergency appears on the wire, something of major importance, chances are the machine will ring. In that case, you rip the page off, rush to a terminal, and type up a "flash," which is about a sentence long, which you precede with this "bells" code so it will ring in Paris when you send it off. Are you with me?"

"So far, so good."

"Okay. You follow up by a "bulletin" which is about a paragraph or two long. After that, you can go into further depth, further detail. If it's top breaking news, like the release of the hostages, you call someone else, because it's too big an event for anyone to handle alone."

I nod, glad to hear some of the barely digested notions of the two previous weeks reinforced in the night's more peaceful atmosphere. The voice is less condescending.

"Oh, actually, before any of this, before you set foot in the office, you're supposed to buy the early version of the Washington Post. There's an old guy down at the Hilton who sells it. Like parking, however, it's not reimbursable," he says with a peculiar smile erupting from the left corner of his mouth revealing teeth which remind me of young corn kernels and that seem to have been filed.

I take the elevator down, walk to the hotel a block away, notice that the air has gotten colder. The old news vendor seems a relic from another era. There he is, his back against the wall, wrapped up in a big black duffle-coat, with an apron on top, staring down at the ground, a felt hunter's hat concealing most of his face. I could picture him shouting the news in a James Cagney film. Not as a young man though; he looks as though he had been old in the 30s. Old forever.

"Post, please."

"Twenty five cents," he says like a train conductor announcing a new station. "Thank you and have a good night."

I walk back to the office. To the left looms the YWCA, to my right a huge car is parked. Chrome radiator, tail fins. I look at the name plate: Edsel.

"Let's see what we've got," Pétard says as I return, looking over the headlines then turning to the editorial page. "Hm, nothing terribly interesting. While I think of it, have you done any follow-up stories?"

"Yes, a couple."

"Okay, good. Usually, there are not too many of those at this time of night. That's more for the day shift. You've got to beware though, because certain sessions of Congress go on forever and some of the resolutions are important to report."

All this talk about importance fills me with dread, yet at the same time an exciting feeling of responsibility sweeps over me. They can count on me. I nod.

"So you see how this office operates? Watch out for Mouluvert. He looks okay on the surface but he's the biggest, the coldest son of a bitch you can imagine."

"Is he?"

"He's a top-notch journalist but as a man he is totally heartless. Hertzen, on the other hand — also an excellent professional — is very human. If you have a problem, talk to him, not Mouluvert."

"I would have thought the opposite."

In the meantime, the AP is continuing to crank out more copy.

"Remember now, you can only use news based here in the United States... Let's see what we've got here. Looks like those asshole communists are taking a licking in Afghanistan, just what they deserve. Sons of whores."

It seems as though he is talking more to himself than to me. I feel like a child. One begins to get a sense of superiority at the end of grade school only to be put in one's place in junior high. The same thing happens all over again in high school. Hair pursues its upward ascent on your chest and face and tremulous sensations shoot up and down your body to prove that you are a creature of sexual desires. In America, you are allowed to drive at 16. 18 in France. College follows. What could be more adult than a pre-graduation senior? Hell, now you can vote, order liquor anywhere, go to war, go to jail, and get married, and then: BING! You are tossed into the big real world only to find out you are back in the crib without a tit to sink your teeth in. I could use one, or actually two of those right now. The image of blonde Deborah enters my mind. All hope is not lost.

Pétard skims through the copy.

"A good thing to work on this time of night, where you can hone your skills," he says, nibbling on his lower lip, "are the anecdotal items; peculiar things that happen. There's always a good niche in the market for that."

He suddenly breaks out into his manic giggle.

"Hey, here's one about a guy who got stuck up someone's chimney, claiming he was trying to escape a group of assailants. Bear in mind that you're addressing an international, non-American audience, people who are not interested in too much local detail that AP joyously slaps on to every story. As a matter-of-fact, three-quarters of the AP stuff could be chopped off and no one would be the worst for it."

I settle behind one of the big VDTs and start working on a French version.

"Okay, you're getting the knack of it," Pétard says looking over my shoulder a quarter of an hour later, "but avoid repeating words. It's very simple really, it's like a crossword puzzle grid that you have to fill in. You'll discover how it's very repetitive work in the long run."

Better than washing dishes. No steam to cloud up the old glasses anymore. No grease on the forearms or in the hair.

The seven or so wires, including the Associated Press sports and economics wires that use the carrot-smelling paper, the UWS Spanish and English versions, are diligently typing away. Tic-a-tic-a-tic-a-tic-a-tic. I feel as though I have been plunged into the eye of the news, caught in a challenging media crossfire. So that's what's happening in Beijing. And in Caracas, Rio, Buenos Aires, Calcutta, Tokyo, Ulan Bator, Vilnius, Sarajevo, Pretoria, Port-au-Prince, Kigali, Antananarivo... Hmm. The London stock market headed for a...

DING-DING-DING!

A couple of bells ring out. I react like a fireman smelling smoke.

Michael Kent

"Oh-oh," says Pétard, "that's Paris. They always want you to cover something or other; half the time, they don't know what they're talking about; they're like little frustrated bureaucrats that like to bark up our tree. Some of them have been collecting dust and paychecks in the halls of the Paris office for years and nobody knows about it. They should be fired on their asses. The French system is too lax, there's a lot of fat to cut. Of course, you have to give the more active ones what they want. If not, they get real mad. It can get ugly. Everybody here hates them, from Mouluvert to Vazin. Sometimes we have to remind them that such and such an event has already been covered. Let's see what's irking them this time."

He walks over to the wire closest to the cluster of terminals occupied by the generalists[9] during the day and me henceforth.

"Ah, it's a note for Petitcolis. They want something about the citrus crop in Florida. I'll put that on his desk."

Above which is pinned a most leggy Angie Dickinson advertising citrus fruit. My stomach is reminded that it is not quite full.

Time flutters by; the main AP wire remains quiet. Pétard is at a desk, drawing a 1960s MG. Similar to the one I saw parked outside the building as I walked in.

"Nicest car ever built," he states, amorously ironing out the details. "The French haven't produced a first class sports car in years. The Germans are efficient but that's about it. Americans don't have much of an eye for design, neither do the Swedes. God, Volvos are ugly. Boxes, boom-boom-boom. No subtlety, no refinement. I do like the Italians. Now they are true artists."

"How do you feel about the Japanese?"

"They're promoting comfortable sports cars. What the hell does that mean? That's a contradiction in terms. A true sports car is rough; you've got to feel each pot hole in the road."

The night crawls onward. The wire hardly stirs.

"I remember," says Pétard, "pulling a couple of all-nighters in Paris. Can't stand that city anymore. People are so rude, unpleasant. Such a cutthroat atmosphere. I really enjoyed New York though. Now that's a city."

9 - As opposed to the specialists (White House, State Department, Congress, Pentagon...)

Renowned for its charm. Cutthroat atmosphere, coupled with people who quite literally will slit the jugular.

"I wanted to go there after graduation," I say, "but I got the job down here."

"Washington's not bad, but I prefer New York. The women there are something else. A lot more elegant than the Parisians."

Gradually, the sun casts new rays on K Street. A bluish light spreads down the vacant avenue. Cars begin to emerge, taxicabs, buses; people start crawling out of the Metro even though one cannot hear their footsteps, but they seem too tiny to produce any sound anyway.

"Many nights will be like this, but keep in mind the hostages. Oh, another piece of advice: don't get carried away. It's not a good idea to do too much; rather, just be sure you fine-tune what you are working on."

"How many stories a night should I write?"

"About four should be fine."

He looks at his watch.

"Seven twenty-five. Mouluvert should be around soon. I think I am going to call it quits for now."

The big bald boss arrives ten minutes later, full of pep and enthusiasm.

"Hello Albert, how do you do?"

"Hanging in there. I wrote a few stories with the assistance of Achilles Pétard."

Mouluvert glances at the wire, nods. His lower jaw comes out. I stick around until eight as more people start to pour in.

"See you tomorrow," I tell Mr. Mouluvert.

"Have a good sleep!" he wishes me while still skimming through the wire.

"Thanks."

I take the elevator down to the ground floor. Next to this building is a fast food restaurant which I enter and order an orange juice, eggs, and sausage before taking the Metro over to the Pentagon and then waiting for the bus to return to my new home.

*   *   *

It is five after twelve. Pétard has just left. The MG blasts into the night. Is he the real Zorro? There are no other cars on the street. The audible sounds in the Universal Wire Service are no longer human:

Michael Kent

the wires that tick, the main wire that produces a sound akin to a chain-saw nibbling into a log, the neon bulbs up above, and the TV set. A full color one.

I go through the local production that Dido has stamped with the date; read the international copy. "Important that you should get a feel for the UWS style," says Hertzen. Fine by me. So many events pile up in the world in one day. There are a lot of repeats, sequences, follow-ups. A neverending process. A vicious circle. A few "new" details about the 52 hostages. I can understand why the anecdotal stuff sells; it is often more amusing to read and more pertinent to daily existence.

I flip through the Washington Post. No Watergate Scandals tonight.

Crrrank, crrrrank. The master wire growls. I feel I am in a stable and the cows' udders are craving to be milked. Hold on Mildred, let me get my pail and stool. Squeeze, squeeze. Is this any better? I look over the fresh feed. Boring, irrelevant, leave this one for the economics desk. Hm, this is not bad. I lay the smoldering copy on my desk and start to type.

*Atlanta, Georgia (UWS)* — A 73-year-old woman today rescued an 80-year-old man who was being attacked by a young thief. Mrs. Y grabbed the old man's cane and knocked the aggressor six times over the head until he took off.

She and Mr. X both live in a retirement home in Atlanta but did not know each other before the incident. They believe this is the beginning of a beautiful friendship.

"I love her," said Mr. X. "I even bought her a soft drink when all was over. She really knocked the wind out of him!"

Mrs. Y. added that Mr. X, who only weighs about 120 pounds, is "a little fragile thing who could not defend himself."

My eager index finger presses the green "send" button. Off it goes into the wild blue yonder. I flip through the television channels. There is a watchable western on channel five. I peel a banana, put my feet on the desk and enjoy. Should I call my friends outside of Paris? Gaspard Casard, Lessèphe, Victor? Perhaps my parents?

Crrrank, crrrank. Oh, Mildred, not again! I just took care of you. This is good practice for when I have children and have to change their diapers several times a night. No darling, you stay put. I'll take care of the little varmint.

More anecdotal stuff appears. I toss the banana skin into the trash can. Going to the bathroom becomes a source of minor excitement. And danger. What if the 52 hostages are liberated while my pants are still down? What then? I can see Mouluvert hiding his bald skull under a 17th century wig, pointing an accusing finger at me and vociferating: "J'accuse!" And no novelist to defend me this time around. Nah. Me, hopping with my pants around my ankles back to the terminal. The 52 diplomats will probably remain in Iran forever, pig out on shish kebab, marry seven wives each, and live far more happily then chained to some desk job at the State Department. Any other questions?

The telephone rings.

"Hello?"

"Hi, is that you?"

"What do you mean?"

"Oh-oh. You must be the new person."

"Yes. May I help you?"

"Well, as you might have been told they're after me."

"Who? I don't understand, I'm new here."

"Well, you might as well find out, though you probably have suspicions. It's the C.I.A. They have file-records, but they're all forgeries. I'm innocent and I can prove it. But you have to pay close attention..."

"Listen, copy is piling up and I have work to do. I think it's better that you call during the day. Mr. Mouluvert or Hertzen will be delighted to hear about this."

"Thanks for your understanding, but..."

"No problem, goodbye."

The night creeps by. Mildred is quiet for almost an hour but gets rather excited as the clock chimes seven. The sun peers. A new day begins. Mouluvert arrives.

"How do you do, Albert?" He seizes the night production, including my five dispatches. "Okay, very well, see you tomorrow!"

I have survived the first night. I have survived the first night. Alone. Now back to Park Mapletree for new exciting adventures.

*

# IX

# THE LACKING KNACK

A month has drifted by. One month. It feels like a lot more. As though I have never really lived during the day. I work four days and get three-day weekends. Not bad, except that to catch up with the diurnals, to eliminate the stationary jet-lag, I sleep all day Friday and all of the night.

But, the probation period is over and there has been no talk of my leaving the agency. Ha. Hertzen though struck me as rather vague on the subject when I asked him the other morning. Still, the tall blonde administrator, Sibyl, who shares the same office as Batignole, the accountant, asked me for two photographs. I almost went crazy trying to find one of those automatic machines that will take your picture for four quarters. And on the shots themselves I do have the face of a madman, even though Sibyl said she thought I looked good.

Nothing right now quite beats the feeling of seeing my stories return on the international wire. Some mysteriously fall through the cracks never to reappear. Mouluvert explained that certain issues are of far greater interest to Americans than to the rest of the world, even if AP hams them up. Some of my dispatches are edited more aggressively than others. Sometimes the style has been streamlined, other times it seems as though it is one of the jerks from Paris that Pétard was referring to who feels he has to add his two cents, often diluting my prose's initial punch.

Hertzen invariably sides with Paris. He leaves notes in my box now and then with photocopies of my work streaked with red ink, explaining the dos and don'ts. Perhaps it is because of the odd hours I keep, but I most vividly feel the sting of humiliation. There is the agency's way of writing and no other. I thought I had pretty much adopted it, but there is some finessing that apparently continues to elude me.

"Still," I say, "most of my stories do come back and sometimes they are virtually unedited."

"Well," Hertzen responds, "they're not all geniuses over there either."

Hertzen, you flatterer. I should learn to walk on all fours, eat thistles, and carry big heavy baskets leaking barley and oats.

"My God, you missed that new item about the hostages!" Mouluvert screams at me one morning, after the most perfunctory how-do-you-do yet.

"What new item?" I ask, cool as a freshly peeled cucumber. "There was nothing about the hostages last night."

And who gives a damn anyway?!

"I heard it this morning on the radio as I was driving in."

He searches through the dismissed sheets that have piled up in the wastepaper basket. His eye probes like a hawk's.

"There, there, you see! There it is!"

By Jove! The mask of the red death is upon us and me blind; but, honestly, do I really care? LOOK AT ME, YOU LITTLE NIT-PICKING BASTARD AS I KEEP MY FEELINGS TUCKED AWAY BEHIND THE HYPOTHALAMUS! And by the by, why don't you go buy yourself a wig? There's a sale going on I believe on F Street. It is in the paper, three times bigger than anything you will see on Carter, Reagan, or Iran!

"But the dateline was not in the United States," the romantic young lad argued, groping for strawy salvation.

"Yes," he continues with a voice I now discover sounds quite metallic — follow my intelligence, you knave; "but it says here: *"meantime in Washington."*"

Elementary. Allow me to borrow a whetted scimitar. I shake my head with dismay. No! No! A brown curly-hair wig with wrap-around-the-chin sideburns?

"I see." In a tone that has yet to demonstrate that I have swallowed the journalistic bug.

"You have to be extremely careful," he adds, like a fisherman about to slide a hook through a fly's still buzzing body. "Occasionally AP buries the most important stuff toward the end of its dispatches without notifying at the top that it's based in the U.S."

AP turns out to be rather sneaky, would you not say, my bald boss? Velcro sideburns optional. But, by George! I have learned an unforgettable lesson. Private Nostran, permission requested to kick ass.

"Oh," dry-witted under the ears Nostran politely comments.

Permission granted. How about mine first? He stares at me, like a somewhat disappointed father. Is there anything worse?

"We have very important customers who depend upon our services," the metallic voice drones on. "We cannot afford to have the competition, AP, UPI, Reuters, run all over us!"

"I understand." Intuitive lad that I am, I think my northern European-inherited phlegm irritates him. Call it the syndrome of the man who cannot teach a young dog old tricks. If only I displayed signs of excitement, if only my nostrils flared and quivered, if a hint of fire were to flame out of my dark blue eyes, my gone awry bald boss would find something to sink his fangs into; it would not be quite so bad, he might argue with a shrug, preferably external, but I remain cool like the cucumbers that once flecked the Nostran garden.

\*   \*   \*

Away, banished forever from said garden — and others, I am afraid, for at least the next twenty years — I feel like a choo-choo train on a parallel track, glancing with a pinch of salted envy at the rest of society, an Eve-less Adam pouring my forlorn gaze — when I am not asleep — over the beloved kindly Washingtonians I do not yet know. Until two o'clock in the morning, the old Nostran spirit remains undaunted, pugnacious itchy chin up in the air; I feel pretty good; experience teaches one that it is actually the best time to bask in the quiet of the night, to cleanse pores with lemon-lime peace. This is when the first sleep stretches its downy wings, descending like a shower on an August day, the time of dreams, and of escape. That is the time I would go to bed normally. Afterwards, the absurdity, the vacuum, the loneliness, the despair, creep in. One has nothing to cling to. Nothing seems to really matter, everything becomes relativized. The night no longer feels like the night and the day has lost its day-like quality. I feel like Ben Gun, the man the other pirates left behind on *Treasure Island*, with no cheese or treasure but a check at the end of the month and a promise at the end of the night. It would not be quite so bad if I had a good friend. One good friend.

Often I wonder what the day-team is up to. Sometimes I wish I could join Pétard and talk to Mimi and Dido for a chuckle or two. As I once did. Afterwards we could go out for a drink, or a movie, a play, or a concert... I go to work when most people are about to enter slumberland and fall asleep at around ten a.m., seldom sleeping eight hours, usually waking up at around three in the afternoon.

Davey, who is only partially employed, spends half the day running up and down the stairs with a pair of heavy boots. Badaboom-badaboom-badaboom! A veritable thundering of S.S. The cowboys in red shirts division, the Führer's most beloved. Then it is wee-wee time. In my toilet-training days, I recall being taught to aim to the side of the bowl so as to be as inconspicuous as possible. Gronket, on the other hand, sounds like he is aiming a fire hose in the deepest and therefore loudest possible place. I think that even if I tried I could not achieve such a thundering. Thank God he does not have a stereo.

It seems as though he is doing all this on purpose. Of all the roommates, I had to find one who does not work during the day and has too much energy to burn. Can't he choose a park somewhere, buy a cheap bottle of wine, and get drunk?

"KEEP IT DOWN, I'M TRYING TO SLEEP!"

"Okay, okay, but don't forget you owe me seven dollars and 45 cents for the electrical bill."

"Have I forgotten to pay you anything so far?"

"No, but I just want to play it on the safe side," he whines back. "Your predecessor used to drive me crazy."

*Ape* would be more appropriate.

\*　　\*　　\*

Once I have woken up in the afternoon, one of my pastimes is to cross the freeway on the narrow concrete overpass down the street and walk over to Shirlington, a little commercial enclave where some peculiar effort has been made to create the semblance of an old downtown Main Street, something a little less strip-like than average[10]. Only stores, nothing residential. This is where I buy groceries, including the cold pizza with green pepper and pepperoni which I enjoy eating without heating up. Saves on the dishwashing.

---

10　-A more worthy effort materialized in the late 1980s. The location now features first-rate dining, a multiplex movie theater, a couple of handsome post-modern buildings, brick sidewalks...

Last week I bought a lamp with a circular switch to dim the light — something that might come in handy if my social life ever returns from the dead.

As I return to Park Mapletree a feeling of vacuum invades me. Suddenly the world has become a giant freeway. I used to see the asphalt ribbon as the messenger of a new spirituality, the spirituality of tomorrow, equal, nay superior to that of the past. Each bolt, each square inch of tar took on an internal and mystical meaning; each snarling vehicle belching brown smoke stood as a titan of the new era. Then I awoke, and my eye opened up to a utilitarian landscape where gods crouch at the bottom of sterile vaults; I squinted but only to be lambasted by a lack of imagination, the absence of any emotion, and the ugliness that suffocates life and meaning, and I felt the permanent anxiety that several centuries of erosion will not erase.

\*     \*     \*

Having just finished *The Great Gatsby* and now considering myself one of the beautiful people — after all, am I not officially a journalist?! — I scurried last Saturday over to Art Dekkoltey's, a fancy nightclub on one of Georgetown's side streets. I had read about it in the Nightlife guide that I purchased at Kraus's, a lively bookstore a little north of Dupont Circle, which doubles as a café. An island of civilization, the taste of which vanishes as soon as you are out the door.

Between the onyx columns and silver linear motifs that recall the Aztec empire, Dekkoltey's plays a lot of Frank Sinatra and Louis Armstrong. Exclusively slow songs. This greatly favored the initial embrace; but, as soon as I announced that I worked the night-shift, the tall blonde a millimeter away from me, assuming she was ever faintly interested to begin with, slipped away or said something like: "Oh, you should be going out with a nurse, the hours you keep."

Michael Kent

Where are the nurses anyhow? Where do you meet them? Perhaps I should start my own society: *Creatures of the Night, Unite.*

A cliché-ridden youth, I ordered a Martini at the bar. And then another.

Back on the dance floor, a pudgy little thing with a short haircut started to squeeze me. In boa-land, do as the boas. I attempted a lip-landing and an expression of bewilderment shattered her expression.

"What are you trying to do?"

I told her: "If you don't want men making a pass at you, you shouldn't hold them so tight."

"Maybe we could be friends?"

"Fuck it."

Her face collapsed entirely and I took off into the night, singing Brahms's Lullaby.

Christ, am I sick and tired of these women who "just want to be friends!" I have run into them all my life. At least the average Burdon College woman was downright unpleasant. From beginning to end. No movies, no restaurants, no drinks, no walks in the woods, no nothing. They were so cold they did not need refrigerators. Just kept the food taped to their shoulders. No wonder they looked like football players. Down here they are all oh-so-pleasant, but when matters start picking up all they can say is: "let us not get physical, let us remain friends." COCK TEASERS! Despite my monastic life I have extremely secular needs and I see little point in spending money on prostitutes.

The only women I could consider friends would be my mother and other relatives. Of course, there is Gloria, but G-l-o-r-i-a is actually the kind of woman with whom one would only like to be friends. My mother, aunts, cousins, and Gloria. She is quite pretty in her own way; but, not sexy. Not to me. There is Jillian from Richmond, but might as well say Mars, plus she lives at home with her parents.

A woman in a passing Mustang bouncing on the street's cobblestones yells: "Asshole," out the window, after which she collides with a car moving out of a parking space. I get drunk, but you get the accident. Isn't life strange?

\*   \*   \*

When it comes to the dames, Davey is more confident.

"Eventually, I'll have to dump Susan."

Dump? Dump? When they are so hard to get! I look at the framed photograph of a pleasant looking young strawberry-blonde woman on his dresser.

"Why is that?"

"A couple of things," he says, putting down the *Playboy* of November 1966, "for starters, her tits are too big."

I stare at the buxom lass gracing that issue's cover.

"I like them that way."

"You know what they say: more than a handful is just a waste; plus, she's not Jewish."

He was more discrete as to his religious, ethnic, and bosom preferences when Suzy showed up. I expected a bimbo, and although her conversation did not seem to reflect any great intellectual pining, she was warm and friendly, there was something endearing about her around the eyes; and, like a badly married partner who tries to save appearances, Davey had reverted to the charming self I had known before I had moved in. I could understand how women can go back to callous men time after time.

*   *   *

Simon will be flying back to Stone Harbor this weekend for Thanksgiving and so will I. So-will-I. Dum-dah-dum.

Right after work, I waited... and took the subway from Farragut West to National Airport; then, waited... and mounted the shuttle bus to the Allegheny terminal; waited, and flew to Philadelphia on a propeller plane. Outside, the sky was pale grey, preparing for a storm to burst. Struggling against sleep I waited... and climbed on board the plane to Boston where I dozed most of the way. I peered out the window before landing. Weather did not seem to have improved much.

At Logan Airport, I waited... and grabbed the bus heading to the T-Station, where I waited... staring at the light blue and white colors and thought: I am going to the end of the world, I am an alien, not from another planet so much as from another time. You people are diurnal; I am nocturnal. Then the train slid in but I had to switch lines at Government Center for the North Station.

My mother describes the surrounding area under the freeway as being hideous; but, perceived through a Zen eye, as mine was reinforced and trained by my photography professor at Burdon C., I actually relished the industrial gutsiness. There is indeed something very un-hypocritical, very sincere about the brutish art-deco arches and green-painted steel beams fastened together by rivets; perhaps it reminded me of the place I first landed when escaping from Burdon and explored the Hub of the Universe.

Washington is too much of a showcase, sterile; a place needs to be a little rotten to be alive. Down with cleanliness. Up with mold. One of the problems with the U.S. is we have too many clean people while areas like the South Bronx fester in their dilapidation. Compensation. What is repressed at one end comes out the other. I haven't taken a shower in two days and I feel just fine, although few things would feel better right now than getting splashed by a lot of water. Perhaps I will never shower again, perhaps I will stay at the North Station all my life.

Since they are fixing the line between here and Stone Harbor, the train stops at Manchester. I follow the other passengers onto a school bus. On and on and on and on we go. The bus produces a loud sound and reeks of gasoline. We have taken off again. The road winds pleasantly onward, at this point I do not care anymore.

Stone Harbor. At last. Mum and little brother are waiting for me as I get off, with big smiles on their faces. Big smiles where a little apprehension lingers. The Nostran smile. The air is a purple crepuscular blue, similar and yet quite distinct from morning blue which is a prelude to light. I smell the ocean, the iodine, the positive ions. Darkness is falling. Albert Nostran is falling.

"God it's good to see you guys!"

"Oh, my poor darling; you do look tired," says Mum.

Mum's little Rabbit carries the three of us down Broadway, up South Street, left at the Marinader Inn sign, back to Ivanhoe Way. And here is the house, surrounded by leafless trees. The grass no longer is bright green.

"Welcome home, kid," HE says as I step in the door. There HE is, Quentin Nostran, my father. He is wearing the slate blue chamois shirt I bought for him in Freeport, Maine. His pants are a little too big. He looks a little tired, as though he is making an extra effort to present a suitable front. I can detect a mournful glimmer in his blue eyes partially hidden by thick eyeglasses. But, he has spoken to me! This is the first time he has talked to me in two months. *Hallelujah.* It will not be like before, but Pop was never the type to go fishing — which is fortunate since I don't even like fish. Mum's garlic-laden leg of lamb heals ancient wounds. Her outward appearance is chipper and retains the grace and the nobility which force people to treat her with deference.

"Notice anything new?" my father asks.

I look around. There, on the ceiling: a large fluorescent light.

"Looks good."

"It's certainly a lot better than that horrible thing MacFugg left behind," my mother adds. MacFugg, the former owner. I vaguely remember the cheap, ornate, imitation gold of yore.

Winter is almost here. All the tourists have vanished. Like escargots inside their Guggenheim shells. The population of Stone Harbor has shrunk down to a third of what it was three months ago. Our new friends, the Finocchios, have closed down their motel and returned to Malden. A silence, a loneliness permeates the air like in an Edward Hopper painting. Hopper, who painted in this area.

"In Saint-Germain, we were 25 miles east of Paris," Mum says. "Now, we're 40 miles north of Boston. Boston, Boston, they say around here, as though it were the jewel of the crown, some fantastic city. I just see it myself as rather provincial."

"You'll find worse," I say. "At least the streets were traced before the grid-pattern, there are international flights."

"That's about all you can say about it."

"What do you know, anyhow?" my father interjects.

"Come on, don't start," she says.

Yes, don't start. He lets out a small belch and returns to the food while I turn my gaze to the white circle of light humming ever so slightly above our heads.

\*   \*   \*

# All of the Night

I was expecting a few extra swipes but none were to occur. My father has lost some of the old snap; maybe it has something to do with the weather, the isolation. My mother is asserting her rights more. I am also making extra efforts to preserve the harmony but I spend much of the time up in my room with Simon listening to records on the new stereo I bought with clean dishwashing money, just before leaving for the capital city.

"It sounds really good," says Simon, who has never seen it before. He is like a pilgrim at Mecca — "a place in the Middle-East," as a museum docent once told me. The stereo is facing east.

"Too bad it's up here and I'm down there. How's Syracuse treating you?"

"I'm making a few friends but I'm having second thoughts about journalism."

"Why... why, that's impossible!"

He laughs, draws tobacco from a pouch, and rolls a cigarette. Is this the chubby, cherub-faced adolescent who used to look like Paul McCartney?

"Very possible, on the contrary. Just to give you an example. The other day I had to check out some reading on reserve at the library. Okay, I get the book, and guess what? The page I am supposed to read has been torn out."

"Jeeze."

He lights the cigarette; smoke shoots out of his nose. He has placed the pouch on the faded red rug left behind by the MacFuggs. His back leans against the chest on which the amplifier and the turntable rest.

"You know, Simon, you've lost weight."

"Don't drink any Coca Cola anymore."

"Yeah, I noticed. I'm surprised it would make such a difference."

"At least nobody is going to call me 'fat boy' anymore."

"You sound like John Lennon."

"I can relate. Some moron journalist once called him the 'fat' Beatle. I mean, how idiotic! Anything to get the reader's attention. That's what they teach us in Syracuse. Simplify, create narrow categories. And how's UWS?"

"I do like the nature of the job; but, man, I hate the hours. I can understand how the guy who came before me was losing it."

He nods. My fingers trace small trenches in the rug. A couple of tiny seeds get caught under my nails.

"I've never seen you with such long hair," he says. "It looks good."

"Too many people have short hair nowadays. Ronald Reagan has just been elected; it's time to rebel."

I look at the two golden angels nailed on the wall above the bed. One is just a face with wings on either side, the other is a robed, praying figure with closed eyes. A new song starts, for some reason a little scratchier than the last. I look at the turntable.

"It's strange to have a job; you know, I still marvel at the fact that I can tie my shoelaces."

He takes a drag, smiles, shakes his bushy head.

"Yeah; the very act of getting dressed defeats the imagination."

"Tying a necktie is like a major feat."

"I still haven't learned."

"I'd like Pop to teach me how to tie a bow-tie."

Simon scratches his bristly chin. Both angels in fact have their eyes closed. They are out of reach of my bedside lamp's halo. I was most surprised when Pop told me they were carved out of wood. They are golden; how can they be made out of wood?

Below us, beyond my room, beyond Simon's across the hall, beyond his windows and Mum's and Pop's, beyond the shingles, the lawn and the weeds, the ocean growls, lashing against the huge boulder facing the house and the rest of Ivanhoe Way, oblivious to the day and to the night. It remains perpetually restless.

*

# X

# DREAM NUMBER NINE

This time I drove down. In style. In Balthazar, the Mercedes Benz 190 C that has been in the family since 1964. After the accident in the Ford Taunus my father wanted a tank. As Stone Harbor turns into Gloucester and Massachusetts is replaced by Connecticut I remembered how kind and gentle he was these past few days. Our first Thanksgiving in America. Turkey, cranberry sauce, the whole smorgasbord. None of the "you dirty, filthy, no good whore" routine. None of the volcanic rage. The only ashes came from the cigar. The venom was contained or expurgated.

Before I started the big four-cylinder engine he said: "I have something for you," and he gave me a small narrow picture he had painted on the back of a cigar-box, long ago. It represents a silhouette walking with its head down under the stars. He only used two colors: the white to outline the figure and the stars, and the overwhelming emerald greenish blue. I shall hang it up as soon as I return. Right now my walls are bare. The freeway continues.

New Jersey. The Davey Gronket state. A turnpike traced with a ruler. I thought the road would never end. New York City was only the halfway point. Then suddenly I started seeing signs for Philadelphia, then Wilmington, Baltimore, and finally Washington, though I got a little confused on the beltway.

Two tankfuls. Home at last. Duplex at least. There it is now sleeping, parked in our lot in Park Mapletree, next to Gronket's sky-blue Pinto. Pinto: plebeian, and slightly pretentious in its own way. Balthazar, the aristocrat, a work of art. I now have a friend nearby.

"How're you doin'," says Davey, his eyes concentrating on the TV.

"Pretty good. Brought a couple of things down from Stone Harbor."

"Yeah? Like what?"

"A few clothes, my guitar, a painting, a car."

"Yeah? Now is that the Mercedes you were telling me about?"

"Exactly. Do you want to see what it looks like?"

"Okay, let me wait for the commercial."

"I would not suggest otherwise."

We go outside. The air is brisk.

"Pretty nice. It's got some rust."

He can tell these things even when the light dims.

"I'm planning to fix that."

"I like the new models. They're pretty slick."

That is one of the problem of this age. Slick. Sleek. Slippery. No wonder some of the Mercedes's numbers end with SL. Nothing to hold on to. No personality. Strength but no vulnerability. And strength without vulnerability is like the night without the day, black without white, man without woman, the sun without the ozone.

"You received a letter today, by the way," Gronket says.

It is from Ferdinand Latulipe, the mad poet from the Bronx. Once the mad poet from Burdon College. He writes and writes, in his round, all-American handwriting, and seems slightly in love. As he was walking away from the Natural History Museum, he ran into John Lennon. I put down the letter for a second. Lennon! Lucky son of a gun. *I was going to ask him for an autograph but I thought that was a corny thing to do so I just continued.* I read the letter several times. Ferdinand, when good, is excellent.

* * *

"Looks like you're adapting well to the job," Benoit Joffre tells me the second night of my return. He is a relatively tall, skinny fellow with a long nose and black hair who misses the days when the Universal Wire Service was headquartered in New York.

"New York is alive," says Joffre. "Washington... Pff!"

"What about Georgetown?" I ask.

"Georgetown is not bad; it's historic, people do walk around fairly late at night, but it's only a few blocks, no match for Greenwich Village."

Unlike the austere Pétard who seems to enjoy a good and somewhat bitter laugh more by himself, Joffre shares the wealth, adopting phony foreign accents as he goes along.

\*   \*   \*

Last night I produced seven stories. One about a new electronic anti-collision device for airplanes; a second on the arrest of a man who goes around movie theaters to cut women's hair off. "The mad barber strikes again," was my tentative title. It returned on the wire as "False barber but real madman." What are you going to do?

My third story described how the Mafia is disappearing now to be replaced by black and Hispanic crime organizations.

Hertzen returned a photocopy of the latter, specifying that I should have added the "Italian" Mafia and that I should have been more specific.

\*   \*   \*

At Gronket's suggestion I went to the Air and Space Museum, the most visited museum in America. That should have made me suspicious. The Gronk, like a number of other locals, namely Gloria of-the-first-night, seems bent on trying to convince me of the virtues of the area, as though the latter failed to speak loudly enough for itself. *This a real place and a real interesting place too.* Real pretty, real historic. You can't beat that.

Suddenly, left, right, down, and above, I am gliding through a maze of airplanes and space ships, from the Spirit of Saint Louis to the L.E.M. which landed on the moon (in 1969), from a pre-World War II Eastern carrier, the fuselage of which looks like aluminum paneling, handsome and shiny enough for a diner, to the latest jet to break the sound barrier and a few windows down below. Surrounded am I also by loud children and overweight parents sporting colors bright enough lest you forget the additional kilograms that Ronald Reagan, despite his food chain, has decided to gouge.

Funny, before the age of 15 I used to be a real aviation nut, spending hours reading about all the daredevils from Pierre Closterman to Herman Goering; seated at my desk I would glue and paint the airplane models. One day, my friend Damian concocted the brilliant scheme to set them on fire. Nowadays I would rather rest my eyes on a Van Gogh or a Constable. The war inside.

The large-screen IMAX experience did prove compelling. Gronket was right. It does give one the actual impression of flying, making me personally quite air-sick at times. Even though the director did inject a little human touch in the film, it felt too much like the glorification of science. ARE YOU IMPRESSED YET? A Japanese man sitting next to me spent the whole session rustling little pieces of paper. At the end of the show he turned around to the little girl on the row above and handed her two origami birds.

In the basement of the National Gallery I ran into two men and two women from Burdon. For a couple of minutes we marveled at what a small world this is.

"You should marry a nurse," one of the women said to me after I told her about my job.

You should not marry, unless you and your husband promise to get sterilized beforehand.

"The Burdon Club of D.C. is throwing a party in a couple of weeks," the other woman says, "would you like the directions?"

"Er, let me get a pen."

"Here's one."

I walked over to the West Wing to explore the El Greco section. To whom my father devoted a very good article. The room itself was empty. The neo-classical palace was mine. I looked around, dizzy, fascinated, bewitched, charmed, captivated, entranced, enchanted, mesmerized. The rich silver and black tones streaking the Toledo sky, those long bearded Spanish hidalgos... Any one of these paintings is worth a thousand airplanes and the bloody room is empty! Good, more for me.

\*　　\*　　\*

And then.

And then John Lennon.

Eleven p.m. I arrive at the office. Hervé Douanel is watching the television, getting ready to leave.

"Nothing much is happening tonight," he tells me, stretching his arms out, when the program is brusquely interrupted by a solemn voice: "JOHN LENNON HAS BEEN SHOT. His body has been rushed to the hospital."

"Oh my God! Jesus!" The short, tense, seldom-smiling yet amiable Douanel rushes over to the nearest VDT and his fingers machine-gun a flash. Tic-a-tic-tic-a-tic. "This is big," he almost yells. "AP hasn't announced anything yet. The wire is going to ring any second."

"God, who would do a thing like that?" It came out like one syllable.

I was waiting for the big story. In my mind it was something like a typhoon, a hurricane, a fire, an earthquake destroying some big and ugly American city with few casualties. The release of the 52 martyrs. But this? Not John Lennon! Not John Lennon!

"Okay, Albert, could you go to the library and get the Lennon file?"

"You got it."

I rush past the coffee-maker into the small room where the archives are stored and find information on the Beatles circa 1965. Nothing more recent.

After the initial flash, Douanel types out a bulletin.

"Do you know anything about Lennon?" he asks me.

"You bet. I was a big fan. I've read everything written about him and the Beatles."

"Great. This is going to help a lot, because as you can tell most of the files' stuff is crap."

Minutes crawl by. The Associated Press is attempting to catch up. The phone rings. I answer it.

"Hello? This is Pierre Legris in New York. You guys just hear what happened?"

"Sure did. Wearing our fingers to the bone."

"Nasty stuff. I'm going over to Central Park West. I'll give you a call if anything new comes my way."

Just say he ain't dead, man. I am having trouble breathing. Make it, John, make it. Songs flood my brain. Then the TV turns to the Dakota building, the scene of the crime, and a journalist, ashen-face, announces that Lennon will not make it, that Lennon is dead. Lennon is dead. The words do not seem to fit. Wake up and start all over again. Shot by a Mark David Chapman, a disappointed fan. Who had obtained an autograph from the ex-Beatle a couple of hours earlier. Son of a whore.

"That's the fucker who should be shot," I say.

They show Chapman's picture on TV. A bland, American face with a mop of hair covering the forehead.

"Too bad they didn't get Yoko instead," Douanel whispers.

"In more ways than one. At least the pain would have inspired him to write some beautiful songs."

Douanel smiles. He looks sleepy.

"You should write a round-up, an in-depth piece and sign it."

Sign it like my diurnal colleagues. Like the big guys. Like a 20-year old general during the French revolution. I have just been promoted.

I type away. Douanel writes a follow-up. The AP spews out more copy. The television shows a candle vigil starting outside the Dakota building; thousands are singing Beatle songs.

"Okay," says Douanel. "I think I'm going to take off; I'll let you hold the fort. Take care."

The world has been shattered. A keystone in late 20th century culture has crumbled. The Beatles will never get together again. Never-never. We have entered the Reagan era so Lennon had to disappear. The young die to fertilize the old. There seems to be a cruel logic there somewhere. The sixties are buried for good now. I flip on the radio. Almost all the stations, from the classical to the soul, are playing the Beatles or Lennon solo. "Starting Over," "Imagine," "Strawberry Fields Forever," "I Am the Walrus," and earlier songs such as "No Reply" and "I'm a Loser" fill the vacant space. When Lennon sings, he plucks the string deep inside; you can sense exactly what he is feeling, the love, the tenderness, the melancholy. My dispatches have reappeared on the international wire. Verbatim. Take that, Hertzen. Paris has called several times.

"We need the reaction of the American press."

"It's too early, but I'll be getting the New York Times in a couple of hours."

My signed piece, my three-screen piece, a premiere, however has yet to reemerge. Fuck. I think I might have waxed too lyrical. I was no longer typing, I was playing, the words must have turned to music. Fuck them, those assholes in Paris, in Washington, New York, everywhere and anywhere.

My pen wanders and draws the Lennon face with the little round glasses, the hooked nose, thin lips, a face I have drawn many times. Since I was 13. Death is one of those things you tend to forget about. Beyond funeral parlors and graveyards, there is little indication of it to the naked, western eye. For a while it ceases to exist. I throw in some hair and a guitar. I add George, Paul and Ringo. Ringo the vulnerable, like Charlie in the chocolate factory; Ringo the child with the precarious health. Ringo, flying from England. Ringo, which means apple in Japanese. Lennon was coarse and rough. In some ways he did not sing quite as well as McCartney but his raucous voice rang with the same pain, the same madness as Edvard Munch's brush.

It is now eight o'clock. "Dream Number Nine," comes on the station I am listening to. The front door opens.

"How do you do?" Mouluvert asks.

"Lennon's dead."

"Pff. I heard it on the radio coming over. He sort of got on my nerves, he and that Japanese wife of his."

Why Mouluvert, Pétard was right, you are a bastard.

"I think it's a pretty sad day."

Mouluvert glances at the night's production.

"You've been working hard I see."

"It's a big event."

\* \* \*

Hertzen, whom I have not seen in some time after greeting me, says he would like to talk to me about my stories.

"Not to worry," he adds as a look of concern distorts my facial features. "I am generally quite pleased."

On the other side of the room the radio is playing "Instant Karma."
*And we all shine out*
*In the moon, in the stars, in the dark*

\*

# Michael Kent

# XI

# FAVORITE NUMBER

T hirteen: my father's favorite number as well as the number of stories I sent out last night. More than twice as many as the average day person! Most of them reappeared on the international wire. A good sign.

I felt relaxed, self-confident, perhaps because I was not alone. A very nice chap is now manning the computer operation in the other room behind the glass window. A black man with a beard, a bit of a receding hairline, and eyeglasses. We did not talk much but we appreciated each other's presence. Even though he fell asleep around three.

"That way I can do my day job as well," he explained to me before nodding off.

It was 9:15 when I finally left the office. Later than usual. My windshield was coated with ice. I managed to scrape some of it off with a key but drove slowly back to Park Mapletree. I could barely see the road in front of me.

After a few hours of sleep I hear a rap on the front portal. Can a man not get his beauty's rest? I slip on a pair of pants and a t-shirt, slide my fingers through my hair which is standing straight up, walk down the stairs and open the door: it is a young woman.

"Hello, my name is Charlotta Williamsburg. How are you today sir?"

She looks a little like Jane DeBaal, a Burdon professor I got to know better than most, though not quite enough to my liking. The eyes, the skin, the hair are all very dark. She is polite and shy like Jane. Her stature is smaller though.

"Fine, and you?"

"Quite well, actually. I was wondering if I could take a few minutes of your time, because I have an offer that you will find difficult to refuse."

"Oh yeah?"

I look at her. She is pleasantly plump with attractive facial features.

"Have a seat," I suggest.

"Thank you."

She sits on the sofa. I settle down next to her.

"What are your favorite magazines? I have a fantastic deal here for you."

"Actually, I'm not much one for magazines I must warn you."

With television, they are responsible for killing books.

"Oh, come on, I'm sure we can find something here for you. Let me see, oh, all men like to read Esquire."

I nod, moving a little closer to her. Jane let me move closer too.

"How about... Car & Driver?"

"I do like cars."

"They have very well written articles and a good sense of humor."

"That's true; I sometimes browse it in the supermarket."

Our legs are touching. Like Jane's and mine once touched.

"Well, what do you think?"

Her breathing has gotten heavier. She is still attempting to sound the cold professional but her breathing has gotten heavier. I wrap my arm around her.

"Now, now," she says, not terribly convinced.

"Now what?"

The fragrance! It is virtually Jane's fragrance, the smell of animal desire that drove me wild barely six months ago. Grrrr.

"Oh come on, you must have a girlfriend and what will she think if she sees you doing this?"

"I do not have a girlfriend. I WORK NIGHTS."

Grrrr.

"Still, I find that hard to believe that you don't have a girlfriend."

Her eyes look down while the rest of her head moves up. Our lips meet. Tongues follow, making a lot of different organs very happy at the same time.

"It's true."

"So, shall I put you down for Esquire and Car & Driver?"
"Okay."
The form I am looking at indicates that I am free to cancel my subscription whenever I want to. Good.
"That will be fifty dollars and you can pay later."
That should get me a life's subscription.
"I'll do that."
"I should be running along now."
"See you later."
The future is looking a little brighter. Or at least more carnal.

\*    \*    \*

Thirty minutes. That is about how long I lasted at the Burdon College Alumni Club get-together. After spending about the same amount of time trying to find a place to park in Mount Pleasant, a mostly residential neighborhood, not terribly far from the zoo.

What are you doing, what are you doing, what are you doing questions buzzing all over the place. Making it, making it, making it. College is not a place of higher learning, but a stepping rung on the corporate ladder. Who gives a damn about Plato, Hegel or Thomas Mann? The important thing is to keep that smile screwed to your face, feign relaxation and togetherness, and impress the living hell out of your *friends* (though I suspect clubs outside the District of Columbia's chapter to be more congenial). The fact that I showed up there shows how desperate my social life has become.

Oh, one little amusing anecdote. Drisela Hawkins, a tall, in some ways attractive young woman, born it seems with the air of a seductress although she is not one, got mugged on her way here. I somehow remembered her as a particularly unsympathetic character. Even at Burdon, her tall stature and arrogance made her stand out. And she got mugged. An inner smile soothed my festering intestines.

The dishes she brought along to this apparently pot-luck occasion had fallen on the sidewalk, which was not a tragedy since she probably was not a very good cook; besides, while the content lay strewn among the weeds, awaiting the rats, the containers themselves appeared not even chipped.

And when the policeman asked her questions about what the aggressors looked like, she mentioned something about her "peripheral vision." The policeman looked at her as though to say: "just tell me what they look like; who gives a damn about your fucking peripheral vision!" The woman has gotten mugged and she talks about peripheral vision.

I think she could tell I was not perhaps as dismayed as all the other thoughtful souls because she gave me a rather asinine look. Like in the olden days. As blood poured out of the hole in the middle of her forehead, like wine from the hole in the barrel. The policeman was fed up with her peripheral vision.

\*   \*   \*

The electric clock I bought with Davey during our honeymoon days is reading five-to-twelve. It is a small, off-white device which makes a little humming sound. Five-to-twelve. Not a bad time, mind you, as good a time as any; but, I have to be at work in precisely five minutes and it takes me, now that I have the car, 20 to get there!

I have neither showered nor shaved. Not even brushed my teeth. I pull the first available sweater over the mildly odorous sweatshirt I have been sleeping in. One of the nice things about this job is I do not have to wear a coat and tie — until the arrival of the technician, I could probably have pranced around the office naked and jacked off; nobody would have known the difference. Regardless, twice a day — *a day*, so to speak — I do have to exchange minimal formalities with my late-evening predecessor and the early-morning incomers. All of them — and I have double-checked — come fully equipped with nostrils. How well those function is anybody's guess, but this is the sort of chance I am reluctant to take. Except given the exceptional circumstances.

Four to twelve. I storm down the stairs, grab my customary keep-me-going two bananas, and rush outside to the car. Come on, start, old Balthazar.

I whiz down the hill. My foot bears down on the accelerator. Signs flash by. I race like mad up 395 over the 14th Street bridge, past the flashing lights of the pornographic enclave, and then K. I stop at the Hilton, buy the morning "Post" and make it upstairs to suite 400.

That was the beginning.

\* \* \*

At the time, in slight retrospect, I found the incident rather amusing.

"I figured you were running a little late," Pétard says. "Don't worry about it. It happens to everyone."

But after fouling up two leads, my joviality tampered down. My fingered twice pressed the "send" button prematurely, attracted to it like a baby to a nipple. The Paris wire kept on chiming, followed by cantankerous calls. A nasal, anal-retentive voice I had heard once before, said at the other end:

"We don't understand what is happening! What is this artistic blur?"

Maybe you are stupid. Has that ever dawned on you?

"I work as you know from the Associated Press; aside from the television and the morning newspaper, I do not have any other sources; I cannot be inventing things. What can I tell you?"

Click, the phone went at the other end. In one case it was partially the Associated Press's fault for producing an interesting story without the "where" and the "when." Now boys, is that a serious thing to do?

The second story pertained to Lennon. I have gotten into the habit of skimming over the AP wire and this morning I skimmed over some details I should not have. I cannot quite comprehend how it happened. Perhaps the details were just not there when I looked for them, just as the road sign for 395 was not there yesterday morning; the little critters of the house, the little demons work in mysterious ways. The details somehow surfaced when Mouluvert entered the office after a good night's sleep. The skin of a day person glows in a different way and the mind is more alive. Personally my complexion resembles that of a leek or a mushroom.

Now not a morning goes by without the big bald boss finding something wrong. Perhaps I should buy him a box of cigars to humor him. "Beware." Pétard had warned me. Gone is the pleasant Mouluvert of yesteryear. In *Tropic of Cancer*, Henry Miller writes about his blunders as a proofreader in Paris. What his bosses told him about his writing comforts me in my situation.

Hertzen wrote me a month ago: *"Don't use words the meaning of which you do not understand. Avoid too many adjectives."*

Like Shakespeare.

I am probably too used to the automatic, stream-of-consciousness style and have not actually written in French since the token class on Medieval and early Renaissance Literature I took in college a couple of years ago. Christ, I have not lived in France in four years! I never thought it would take its toll. I told Simon that I was glad the job was not artistic, because of the anxieties that art tends to create, the doubts... the ups and downs. I wonder now. I do feel creativity pulsating inside of me. I want to start painting again, combine the technique I learned in college and apply it to the type of surreal fantasy that dappled my high school years.

I have also inherited my father's absent-mindedness. The irony remains that both bosses seemed pleased with me at the beginning. I might be going through a bad period. No woman, a churlish roommate, the night hours. Still, I do not feel particularly bad.

Mouluvert did not scold me particularly harshly today but something in his tone of voice was inferring that I was quite foolish.

"But that was very important! How could you miss it? Paris is furious! We have important clients."

A feeling of shame overwhelmed me from follicle to toenail. But I know that most of my leads are good. Joffre thinks so and Hertzen — even Hertzen — does too. "Most" however does not count.

Tonight I will arrive early. And shower. And shave.

*  *  *

Last night before I left for work the telephone rang.

"Albert? Is that you?"

"Hello Mum."

"Oh, I'm so glad to reach you!"

"What's the matter?"

"Well, as I had mentioned, your father and I went down to New York this week. And you know how he is about cigars. He insisted on going to this store somewhere down on Broadway, and once we were there he fell down a flight of stairs."

"Oh my God."

"It was awful. We took the train back up to Boston and he appeared to be okay then, although he did seem to be in awful pain, so we took a taxi from the South Station up to the house. The shock was not immediately apparent but a couple of days afterwards he became, to quote the doctors, 'confused and disordered.' Apparently he's had a stroke."

"A stroke? God."

"He was put into a hospital room in Salem with a dying man who stinks — poor wretch — to high heaven. Can you imagine that? I'm very concerned and so is Simon."

For all his faults I do love the old man and could not stand the idea of anything happening to him. I remembered how kind and gentle he was at Thanksgiving. I looked at the painting of the lonely silhouette walking under the stars. I hope he is well when I return for Christmas.

Hanging up the phone I feel very empty.

*

# XII

# X-MAS & NEW YEAR

The Universal Wire Service has just wished the world a Merry Christmas. I lift an imaginary glass of champagne then pour the content out on the rug because I have to work. The Paris wire features a large JOYEUX NOEL surrounded by glittering asterisks. Them guys know how to party. I am here, Job, Timon of Athens, Prometheus, Satan, not the fifth Beatle but the 53rd hostage atoning for past sins. In the wastebasket by the desk I spot the remainders of a cake, a few plastic cups. Thanks guys, you should not have left so much, I might get indigestion. Scroom all. I catch myself smiling from the side of my mouth, like Achilles Pétard. One day the two of us should go out somewhere and get sloshed.

The telephone rings.

"Universal Wire Service, how may I help you?"

Is it the editor from Paris who hung up the phone in my face?

"Oh, you're still here?" No, it is Mr. Strange Man with the rotten life story. "On Christmas Eve?" he continues in his whispering drone. "They are pursuing me again. They've discovered something new. See this is how it all happened. It started about thirty years ago, before you were even born probably, at the time I was still married..."

I had not heard from Mr. Strange Man for a couple of weeks and did not particularly want to.

"Merry Christmas to you too," I said, "but, as I am sure you're aware, duty beckons; so, good night!"

I tried to make it sound cheerful.

\*   \*   \*

Not one, but two pink slips are fluttering on Balthazar N. Benz's windshield, tucked under his left windshield-wiper. Not biodegradable but coated with plastic to survive storms and nuclear meltdowns. This is not the first time. At the beginning, I left the car — if I dare refer to Balthazar as such — next to a parking lot in the back alley, between the office building and the fast-food joint, only to find my German-mobile one day blocked off by a (Chevy) pickup truck.

Bastards.

"You shouldn't park here," the parking attendant told me.

"But I work from midnight to 9:00 in the morning, and don't get paid for parking. And, the lot is locked."

He looks at me. Not an unintelligent look, actually a rather reasonable look. An American look: no problem is big enough that it cannot be solved. I am more French: certain things cannot be resolved, nor should they be.

"We can cut a deal..."

I am suspicious of deals. Moreover of cutting.

"No thanks," adds the journalist in need of a shower, bed, and even a shave were it not for the fact that he will have to wait another good, good so to speak, eight hours for that. "I'll take my chances and park in the street."

"Okay, just tell me if you change your mind."

There are a lot of things I wish to change on this planet but "my mind" does not come close the top of my priority list. You change your mind, Mister, and I will change the kitty litter which my roommate mistakes for the boy's room. What is the sense in arguing?

Moreover, the meters start at 7:00, which means that I have to leave the office to feed their voracious appetite. Assuming I have enough quarters. The hostages, my God; what if they are released from their chains and I am gone? Why do I not get a parking allowance? Mouluvert, explain that! The day people can rely on public transportation, but with my schedule the waits are so long.

I shove the pink ticket in my pocket. Thank goodness I have Massachusetts plates.

\*     \*     \*

The following morning, I managed to catch a direct flight to Boston. Exit Philadelphia bullshitum. I parked Balthazar on a muddy lot at Crystal City and then hopped on the Metro to the airport with my small backpack, praying the car would still be there when I returned.

It was lovely to be home again, gazing at the ocean, speculating on what lies on the other side. The house with the baby-blue shutters has acquired a certain warmth over the months, the Saint-Germain objects, the Nostran touch is beginning to take root, gather dust.

Yet the atmosphere was also tinged with anxiety and sadness. My father was away from the little fun Mum, Simon and I shared, stranded with a broken ankle and a confused mind in the intensive care unit of the Gloucester Hospital, which, in good taste, has been erected next to a graveyard.

During my three-day stay we drove out to visit him three times and each time I cried. Though his mind might have appeared somewhat adrift, I had not seen such kindness, such innocence in a long time.

"So what are you doing these days?" he asked.

There he lay, propped up on a pillow. His blue pajamas now seemed a little too big for him. His chest did not barrel out as it used to. Last time I had seen him in a hospital bed was in Paris, a few months after Simon's birth. After he had crashed the Ford Taunus, before buying Balthazar. His forehead was streaked at the time by several parallel rows of brown stitches. They looked like barbed-wire. "I bet you're sorry I'm not dead," he had told Mum. The man in front my present eyes was a frail creature, a sweet little boy.

"Commuting from Washington to Boston."

"God, such exciting places."

I smiled. Still the snob, the world-traveler, scornful of the two humble yet pretentious extremes of the East-Coast megalopolis. A few electric words emerged from the little black-and-white television set which my mother bought him a week ago and which the nurse has set up on a shelf.

He had difficulty breathing and every time he caught his breath I could feel my own throat tightening.

"How are you?" I asked.

His lower lip curled up, a mannerism he once told me was typically French. He had very little in common with anybody from the Massachusetts North Shore or any American I had ever met. Gone was the violence, the aggressiveness, the machismo, the unpleasant traits that in some ways gave him energy to live. A chicken in Britain survived a whole month with its head chopped off. He lay on the bed, more subdued, a blend between a wise man and a child. Simon and I held his still powerful, freckled hands, and took turns caressing his white hair.

This absolute of evil — the man who called my mother a whore, a flea-brain, even a lesbian (in 1974); Simon a bastard; me a turd; and threw shoes after Goblin the cat as a warm-up exercise — was also the absolute of good. A complete man. He spoke with a soft, gentle voice. I could quite literally see, feel love glowing in his kind, myopic gaze. Such a proud man, now helpless, frail, called "Quentin" by the insolent nurses. I do not think that I ever loved him more than during those precious minutes.

To walk through his studio was like a curious journey into the past, even though he had not much used it really, spending hours reading the Boston Globe on the couch and, then, after a long semi-catatonic spell, reorganizing what the movers had carelessly thrown together, lamenting the fact every time the family settled down for a meal.

"I should sue these damn, no good, sons of bitches!"

Even though the smell of Dunhill tobacco now permeated the quiet air, Nostran senior felt as though the cross-Atlantic trip had wiped away the magic, a certain flavor, a bouquet that 20 years in the French countryside had amorously shaped. The old wine had been transferred from the tranquility of a rotting cask to aluminum efficiency. Pop hated conventional order but seemed to find his own in what the unaccustomed eye would describe as chaos. "Bless this mess," said a cardboard sign he had bought in 1970, hung in bubbly, paisley, psychedelic pinks, purples, and oranges above the door. Beyond the three iron files lay stacks of canvasses, portfolios bulging with charcoal and pen-and-ink drawings, hills of poems, mounds of yellowing articles stamped with footprints, arcane documentation. Nothing much from recent years, except for a big handsome oak table bought at a yard sale in Ipswich. Blocking the way in the middle of the room, it is suffocating under more paper; its drawers though are nearly bare except for the freshly printed business cards and golden labels which read: *Quentin Nostran, 39 Ivanhoe Way, Stone Harbor, Massachusetts.* The telephone number but no zip code. You could almost smell the ink. He had placed his old green iron desk by the window in the corner to capitalize on the better light, the view of the Atlantic, and the rocky shore; but he disliked the fact that people walking down the road could see him at his typewriter.

"I feel like I'm on display," he said. "Like an animal in a zoo or something. Oh, there's the writer, they must think, isn't that quaint?"

With a touch of guilt blended with apprehension, I opened the desk's drawers. I felt like an infantry man snooping through the Führer's bunker. Down below were touches of rust and the blood-curdling squeak of metal scraping metal. A strip of paper here, tobacco crumbs, thumb tacks, paper clips, staples of various sizes, a red and pink (for the face) plastic elf who had escaped from some birthday cake, a good-luck rabbit paw, and a series of passports; one, with a burgundy cover offered a sepia shot, featuring the journalist as a young man in his James Joyce/John Lennon period. Beyond greying and loss of hair, beyond the wrinkles was the transformation of the eyes. In the beginning, on the sepia photograph, one could see hope, dreams, energy, good looks; the following, black-and-white period, displayed a certain roguishness, not to say cynicism, a sounder knowledge of life, perhaps even better looks, bushier eyebrows as well; in the end: color, regrets, and an attempt to smile.

Tremors rose inside my body, I had difficulty breathing. I peered out the window. No one today to gape at the writer in the creative process. The staring crowd has sought shelter down south or by the fireplace, a radiator or television. The sky was tumultuous, grey, purple and black; in some ways far more compelling than what it might appear on a hot summer day — to the eye moved by Constable, Turner, or El Greco. The studio had been a determining factor in buying the house and now it seemed that he would never use it.

The last time I saw him was Sunday. Only one of us was permitted to go, and since Simon was remaining a couple of extra days, I chose to be the one.

"My, you look handsome today!" he exclaimed as I entered the room. "I hear you are really working well in Washington. Mama and I are very proud of you."

He said nothing but warm, sensitive things, knowing, it seemed, that his own golden days were behind, a thought he had never learned to accept and one of the main sources of his bad temper. I shall never forget the smile on his face when I departed: the smile of someone who loves and feels he is loved, a smile which meant that he placed all his trust in me. A smile of eternal peace, contrasting with his previous threats to kill me and the feud which my leaving for Washington seemed to have ended. For that I am grateful. Like a congressman, I had to return to the seat of government.

Where Balthazar awaited in the muddy lot in Crystal City.

\*　　\*　　\*

I called my mother up tonight. She is very deeply affected.
"The doctors say that your father will never be able to return home."
"God."
The home he has built and ripped apart. The perfect Blakian figure whose antagonistic achievements annihilate one another. Never. The biggest word of them all. My father fought the battle of Ahab. Baudelaire attempted a similar fight, the quest of the *honnête homme*[11]: combat *the never* so that posterity may treasure your scintillating wounds. They of course never heal — the never-ending decay of bloodshed which humans spiritually inherit and would be foolish to disavow, they cannot and must not.

---

11　-Literally, the honest man, but actually, the aristocrat.

Fast food and Sunday-afternoon football are attempts to escape. Many seek refuge in mediocrity. Mediocre humans do not know or care or think they care about what they are missing but no one can eternally flee the dichotomy which splits the world. Like two-faced Janus, we were born to laugh as well as to cry; some external force sees that the equilibrium between the two is maintained. Those who possess the knowledge, the force, perceive the deficiency. Father possesses the knowledge, he has stolen the fire from the Gods.

"He called your name, asked for you specifically," Mum tells me.

The news fills me with more grief. A subtle pain crawls up my body. I wish I could help him, I do not want him to suffer. Perhaps Lennon was lucky to get shot at 40. I put the receiver down and walk slowly upstairs to my room.

*   *   *

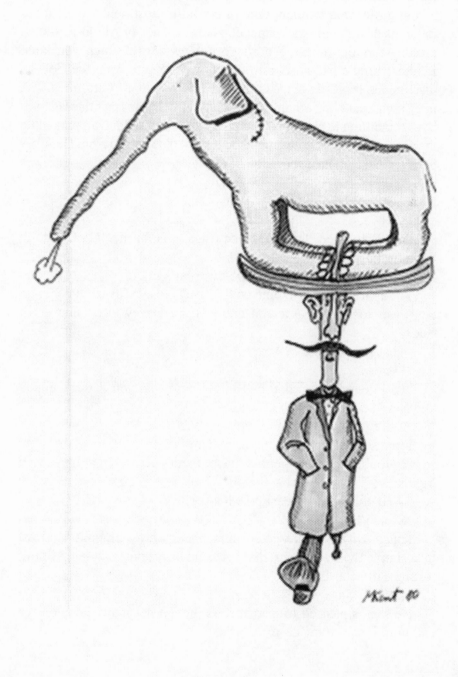

I have just met a couple of Burdonites to catch a movie. "The Border," with Jack Nicholson. He plays a customs officer who helps a young Mexican woman. One of his best, most noble roles. Ideas rattle inside my brain like paper clips inside a box of Altoids[12]. Rattle, rattle. After the movie, we all go our own way. Catch you later. Like catching a bar of soap in the shower. Where were the College discussions of yesteryear? Only in New York with Latulipe '79? I pour my paper clips down a nearby sewer hole. At least the rats will have something to chew on. Then I walk back to Balthazar, parked up the avenue in a most convenient location, a block away from DeSalles Street, where I notice the ABC building.

*   *   *

Park Mapletree. The telephone rings, it is for me, it is Charlotta Williamsburg.

"Are you doing anything for New Year's Eve?"

The apartment is dark and cold. Davey believes in saving energy. I go over to the radiator and crank it up. Davey also believes in sharing.

"That's tonight."

"I know."

"I'd like to, except that as I might have told you, I work nights and New Year's Eve is no exception."

"Can't you get anyone to replace you?"

From shy saleswoman to pushy date.

"I doubt it, most people have made plans. Imagine, New Year's Eve."

"Well could you at least give it a try?"

"Sure, I'll try."

I put down the phone, go upstairs, put on a sweater, light the stove by a simple twist of the wrist, throw some eggs on a pan — psshhhh — and call Pétard.

"Hey, how are you?"

He seems pleased to hear me, as though not many people ever call him. I expose my case.

---

12   -"The originally celebrated curiously strong peppermints."

"No, I'm sorry. Everybody books New Year's weeks, even months ahead of time."

"I understand." Even though I do not ever do much "ahead of time." "Ahead of time" is an alien and even threatening concept.

I call Charlotta back and tell her:

"I only start work at midnight, which means that we could spend the evening together anyhow."

She pauses.

"Okay. I'm in Falls Church. Can you come and get me? I'm at Ling Fu's; it's a Chinese restaurant."

I look out the window, snow is now pouring down like feathers from a pierced pillow. I look at the dead apartment. The cadavers of dead furniture streak the rug. The stench of dust-blood makes one want to sneeze.

"Fine."

The good thing is that there are not too many vehicles on the road; the bad thing is that this Chinese restaurant seems to be quite literally in China. Mile after mile after mile goes by. The windshield wipers are doing jumping-jacks in the Himalaya and are going to have to get paid overtime. At least they are working. I do not recognize anything. Such madness. But in suburbia there is actually nothing to recognize, except if your name is Davey Gronket. Like many a newcomer I was under the impression that it did not snow south of New Jersey.

After making a couple of wrong turns I arrive at Ling Fu's, get out of the car, look around and around and around. Only the tall street lamp up above indicates that I am still on Planet Earth.

"Is anybody here? Charlotta?"

No one is there. Thanks for the wild goose chase. There is certainly enough down on the ground to prove it. I get back into the car, drive back, do not get lost. Snow is still coming down.

I have barely walked in the door that the phone rings again. Always give the other the benefit of the doubt.

"Where are you?" she asks.

"Me? Where am I? I went out to Falls Church and you weren't there!"

"I know, I had to run an errand, but we must have just missed each other. I'll be there this time."

JESUS.

But the alternative is staying at home. I do not feel like reading or watching any green television, so I take off again. The snow has calmed down a trifle but the restaurant is as far as ever. I should start a shuttle service.

There she is, covered up in a thick plaid coat.

"Hi," she says in a weak voice, demonstrating about as much enthusiasm as someone who has driven twice from Park Mapletree to Falls Church under heavy snow. She waits by the car for me to open the door. I do. We take off.

"Do you think the 52 hostages are going to make it home soon?" I ask, trying to liven matters up a bit.

She shrugs her shoulders. My God, woman, do you realize how important the bloody hostages are?

"Nice car," she says. "Do you have a radio?" she stares at the chrome-plated 190 on the dashboard where the sought-after contraption should protrude.

"I'm afraid I don't."

Rule number 27 B, paragraph F: a car is a good start but you must own a radio. I guess she is not wild about the fact that the heating in the car seems a little deficient these days or that I must work after 12:00. Does that mean that she wants to...?

"Here we are, Park Mapletree," I announce.

We walk towards the front door, trudge through the freshly fallen snow.

"Do you want to come up to my room?" I ask. "There's nothing much down here. Besides, it's warmer."

Davey is a miser but I am not against conserving energy.

"Okay."

Welcome to the room with nothing on the walls except for my father's little painting.

She sits down on the bed and I join her. We begin to make out. She kisses nicely, a sweet velvety tongue, but her breasts and the rest of her sag lifelessly. I throw a jazz tape on my small Telefunken cassette recorder.

*Every day, every day, I get the Blues...*

If only I had my big stereo instead of it going to waste up in Stone Harbor. It would help, but I feel strangely uninspired. Rule 28: women are not interchangeable. Rule 29: men are not always in the mood. Rule 30: certain external events may transform the most passionate lover into a block of ice.

"I've got to go to work," I say, "but you can spend the night here."

"Okay."

Still lying on the bed, half undressed, she looks at me with a mixture of what I interpret to be resentment and admiration. For once, I am glad to go to work. Or at least to the office. A third time, I plow my way through the night. The Washington Monument, the Capitol, the Lincoln and Jefferson Memorials are all lit up, isolated from the rest of the world, the rest of the United States, the rest of the capital.

I am glad to go to work. Or at least to the office. The technician is not there and the wire is even deader than on Christmas Day. I type a couple of short pieces, then go to the front of the newsroom where some wise interior decorator once installed a couch. I am tired of busting my ass to be scolded by Mouluvert. I cannot start the new year with a bang so allow me to get some rest. If a major event breaks, the AP buzzer will jolt me anyhow.

I wake up a couple of hours later, look through the copy. Remarkably little has piled up. All quiet on the Middle-Eastern front. The infidels do not believe in the Christian calendar. The 52 prisoners will have to wait a little longer. Before they admire the snow-capped peaks of the District of Columbia.

The 14th Street Bridge is coated with sleet and the rear-wheel driven Balthazar pulls an involuntary U-turn. My heart leaps to the front of my incisors. Lord have mercy, there are virtually no other cars in sight. I pull a second U-ie and resume my itinerary over the semi-frozen Potomac, back to my abode.

There she is, Charlotta Williamsburg, snoring peacefully away in my bed, wearing my grey Burdon College sweatshirt. I tap her on the shoulder.

"Do you want some breakfast?" I ask.

"No, I'm okay. I've got to meet a friend at Ling Fu's."

Good.

A third time I drive to Falls Church. The snow has stopped falling; the roads are fairly clear. I discover the region in a new, more poetic light. A pickup passes us on the right. Although this is only a two-lane road.

"Get out of the way, asshole!" the driver yells, ignoring the rest of me.

"Fuck off," I reply, not wishing to start a fight.

There is life beyond the Press Agency, beyond green television, beyond Davey Gronket, beyond the Mall, beyond the Potomac. I can feel my northern European blood bubbling inside of me. My nostrils tingle with pleasure.

I pull into the parking lot, stop the car by a pair of abandoned chopsticks and spilled frozen carry-out chicken and cashew nuts.

"Can I come and see you again?" she asks.

In light of our fascinating conversation not to mention the 100 miles or so I drove under hideous conditions I tell her:

"No. With the night job that will be impossible."

"Okay."

She nods, gets out of the car. I feel a little sorry for her but also relieved driving home, though I cannot sleep. Should I have picked up the chopsticks? A little Chopin on the radio helps me get by.

*

## All of the Night

On the fritz
We both are
How lovely!
I shall fly
With you
*Compagne de misère*
And enjoy your
Coat of arms monocle
Which dapples
Your red wink

Moist-
The word almost hisses
Almost
Like air escaping
A smooth punctured tire
The wheel wobbles
Whirls, wriggles
We shall fly
You and I
Volare!

To fly
To die
A little sand in between
Flattened out
Or, in a womanly bottle
Together
Hope remains
Shhhhhhhh!

I understand you
You me
Do not die
Together
We shall fly.

# XIII

# GLOWING-GLOWING

Do my eyes not deceive me or has Mouluvert not entered the office this morning with a charming, delectable, yet understated young lass? Several shades of blonde, spanning from ocher to gold, glimmer in her long hair; she is quite tall, has high cheekbones, green eyes, an attractive nose, fleshy lips, no makeup. I like her loose white sweater which cannot entirely conceal a generous bosom, and nicely-fitting blue jeans. Something about her says "let's go camping, let's go prance around in the forest, and dip into a pebbly brook." Dip, not splash, for she seems most delicate.

She is the new copy girl, pretty like a Gainsborough sketch when she is serious and bubblier than a Versailles fountain when she smiles. Her name is Claire. The prince of darkness (me) has met the princess of light. He, thus, is radiant.

After bumping into her every morning, unfortunately not literally, our relationship has evolved from mere recognition into jovial conversation, interrupted by Mouluvert. Trying to flirt behind your wife's back, eh? Naughty boy. Not that I blame you entirely and your reputation for selfishness precedes you, but give the serf a chance. Curiously, Claire seems to like him, sort of as a friend, or a friendly uncle; she giggles at his attempts at humor — for this alone I am not ungrateful, but it is clear that her natural modesty has drawn the line. (Sigh).

\*    \*    \*

Time to buy and install the radio and cassette deck. I drop Balthazar at Schweinhund's, the cheapest outlet I could find, on Glebe road, and ride a bus back to Mapletree.

I am about to unlock the front door when the hideous truth spits right in my eye: hell is murky; I have forgotten the keys to the apartment, left them on the same ring as the car keys. I look around then at my watch: 10:30 a.m. Not exactly the crack of dawn. I knock on the door. No answer. I try a second time. Louder. Ah: those ballerina footsteps prancing down the stairs. Badaboom-badaboom-badaboom.

Davey appears in his pajamas and bathrobe. His eyes are half shut, his hair looks like an old mop.

"So good to see you, old chap!" I exclaim.

Should I embrace him?

"Have you sworn to drive me crazy?!" he responds, mild creature that he is. "I came home last night at 3 o'clock in the morning! I've barely slept a wink."

I shrug my brawn.

"Like I'm supposed to know. That's not my fault."

"Oh yeah?! Have you seen the dishes you supposedly cleaned? They're filthy! Grease all over them. I'm going to get an ulcer!"

Hey, there is always Tagamet or Tums, in case your doctor provides reassuring advice.

"Enough's enough," I retort. "Watch what you're saying! I was once a professional dishwasher."

At the Marinader Inn in Stone Harbor and on the Salamander Ranch in Wyoming. I have letters of reference to prove it. You cocky little son of a bitch. Where the hell do you get off?

"You were?! Well it doesn't show!"

He rushes into the kitchen and produces the battered kitchenware he must have found in a trash-can in Hoboken, pin-pointing how he had to scrape very hard to compensate for my negligence. I admire the work, listen and wait for question/comments/criticism-time.

"I have to give it to you, old chap, you're a better man in the kitchen than I. For crying out loud, Davey, have you gone through college only to be a dishwashing fanatic? A dish critic? Jeeze, I'll replace your crappy, garbage-can dishes, if that's all that makes you happy. As for waking anybody up, man, you take the cake; you're the loudest, most inconsiderate son of a bitch I've ever lived with."

"Tssss. You know something. There's something very weird about you."

"What's that?"

"You sound like an American, but you don't act anything like an American."

"Is that a crime?"

"It's not a crime. It's just weird, it drives me nuts. Like being anti-American."

"Anti-American? Me?"

"Of course you!"

Labels, labels!

"The hell does that mean? Criticism is the root of democracy, you should know that. It's when you start accepting too much that things get dangerous. When I was in high school I got hoarse defending this country; but I'm not going to accept everything on these shores either. This is the land of freedom of expression, remember?"

"And you know something else?"

"It depends what that something else is."

"You think you're so much more intelligent than I am."

"Oh, come on."

"It's true. But really, what can you teach me?"

This conversation is more surrealistic than a Buñuel film.

"Plenty of things. I wouldn't know where to start."

"Yeah?"

"Why don't you go back to bed?"

"Okay."

That morning, I chuckle myself to sleep.

\*     \*     \*

The mail arrives. A letter. A letter for me. A letter for me from Jillian! After a little solitary polka, I call her home in the evening, she is there. Richmond is far but I do not care.

"Would you like to get together next Friday?" I suggest.

"Oh, that's awfully sweet of you but next Friday I can't. How about the following one?"

"Fine."

"I'm looking forward to seeing you again."

"Likewise."

La-la.

\*   \*   \*

"Could you please come and see me in my office?" Mouluvert asks me. The new morning sun is nibbling away at the snow. Sissy snow.

"Okay."

The routine has resumed. I sent six stories over last night, a couple prematurely. That darn send button; it teases the finger.

"Have a seat."

"Thanks."

Mouluvert has not shaved today. Oh, his upper lip and cheeks are smooth enough, but his scalp reveals more whiskers than I actually suspected grew on the lunar surface. His hands are clasped together, he is avoiding my gaze and peering, chin up, out the window. I look that way myself.

"I'm sorry to tell you this," says he, "but your performance recently has left something to be desired and we feel as though we cannot keep you here any longer."

Happy New Year to you too. And how is the missus?

"Suits me fine," I say. "Do you think I enjoy wasting my life working the graveyard shift? Maybe you should give it a try? Okay, so long. You know where to mail the check."

I get up from the chair, feeling a mixture of anger, humiliation, and relief.

"Come, come. Besides, your contract requires you to remain here another *month*."

"Like the month's probation and then what? I don't even like this boring, sterile town. I have no friends here, I have nothing! Besides, if I am so lousy, how can you take a chance like this?"

Give me Paris, London, Rome, where mold spews out from every wrinkled street corner. Away from bureaucracy and the sordid American dream!

"Listen I know how you must feel. It's not really up to me to hire or fire people but Paris was complaining... We do have very important clients. All is not lost. We do have contacts and another month's experience will not hurt. As you know, the pay is not bad."

Insert testicles in vice and turn the lever. One, two, three... Is that tight enough? We can make the necessary adjustments.

\*   \*   \*

I walk out into the street, though the logic of pain would dictate me to look downward, I cannot help but notice the scaffolding surrounding the YWCA.

"What are they doing?" I ask another man watching the spectacle.

"They're tearing it down."

What? This oasis of dignity in this mess of *clean* lines.

"That's crazy! It's the most beautiful building on the street!"

He continues to look as the once venerable structure is turning into a pile of bricks and dust.

"It's progress."

"But it's the right height!"

He shrugs his shoulders.

\*   \*   \*

I walk over to the green television set, flip it on, and watch M\*A\*S\*H\* smiling to see the freezing doctors in Korea while I am freezing my own arse off in Northern Virginia.

"Guess what?" I say to Davey when he returns.

"What?"

"I've been fired."

"What? That's too bad."

"Yeah. I think I'm going to have to leave this place. Besides, let's face it, we don't get along too well."

"I've had worse than you."

"Always the gentleman."

"But I'm going to have to find a new roommate. You're going to have to help me."

"Okay."

\*   \*   \*

Friday morning. Fired up as well as fired, I have written about a black-out in Utah, the most recent Soviet jumbo-submarine, a bale of marijuana ripping through a mobile home in Florida, and a fire in New Jersey — all of which were not only picked up by the international wire but barely modified. There she is, O woman amongst women, cutting the copy. How nicely her fingers clutch that ruler. I walk up to her, gather my courage, and asked her if she wants to see the movie "Raging Bull."

"Sounds good. Who's in it?"

HALLELUJAH! HALLELUJAH!

"Robert De Niro."

"Oh, I love him. I assume it will help if you have my phone number."

Lord, she is pretty. Thank you, Deborah for saying no thank you, Albert, for not pursuing the Williamsburg case.

The next day I call her up. Her sister answers the phone.

"Claire is in the shower. May I ask who's calling?"

"Albert Nostran."

"Oh, my father's talked about you. Okay, I'll have her call you back later."

I put down the phone a little stunned. Her father... that is, the father of one sister has to be the father of the other, that is, Claire's father is MOULUVERT?! I do not know what to think. Of course, it all makes perfect sense. Somehow, I smile. Dating the boss's daughter. The boss who without a shade of a scruple gave me the boot.

A few minutes elapse. I return to the kitchen to scrub the pots and pans. The phone rings. Is it her little fingers turning the dial to call me? Is it her delicate ears waiting for me to respond? Yes. Claire's voice purrs on the other end of the receiver as she gives me directions to get to her house in Bethesda. Maryland. Where I have yet to set foot.

"Just follow Massachusetts Avenue North, past Ward Circle, and you'll be fine."

We chat about this and about that, my colleagues, books, fleeting impressions, like we do at the office, and then hang up.

I leap and yell and dance all over the duplex, feeling the vibrations of a long lost obliterated sense of joy.

A little ashamed of myself, I dunk my feather in my inkwell and write the other woman, the one who came to me, but I shall not hunt two hares at a time.

*Dear Jillian,*

*The job at the United Wire Service is over, my boss has fired me, so I shall return to Boston. I am very sorry but I think it is better like that.*

*Regards,*

*Albert*

\* \* \*

First, I got onto Massachusetts Avenue heading south. Somehow south felt more like north than north. Like left sometimes feels like right. That's where the circles were. At least in my head. Then I flipped the car around, tried Bethesda and I ended up on Wisconsin Avenue. A part I was not yet familiar with. Although a very simple route, I did manage to get lost a half dozen more times, soaring up and down hills at 70 miles an hour, passing other cars where no one has passed before to make up for wasted time, but finally I reached the house, a handsome example of Georgian architecture. A tall thin woman with glasses and an apron opened the door.

"You must be Albert? I am Claire's mother."

"How do you do."

At first she struck me as bland as her daughter is spicy and yet the more I looked at her the more charm I detected.

She led me through a spartan vestibule down a spartan corridor to a spartan reading room. No paintings, no swords, no suits of armor, no bear skins. And there she was, my date, Claire, wearing a black sweater, and a delightful, playful grin, more entrancing than ever.

"Whoa, nice car!" she said when she saw Balthazar.

Driving back towards the city I told her my tribulations getting to her place. She laughed, adding: "I bet you will never get lost again."

Hm.

We followed Massachusetts down to Dupont Circle, found a parking spot. As *Raging Bull*'s black and white images flickered by I felt the urge to kiss her hand. There it was on the armrest next to me. Suddenly, I grabbed it and brought it to my lips.

"I won't think you're weird if you don't make a pass at me," she said.

Not you; please, not you. Sweat sprinkles the screen. It looks more like popcorn being tossed up in the air than water. Pow! Pow! Wham! Pow! Wham! goes the fist, like fingers at a typewriter. Mean old swollen fingers at a mean old manual typewriter. De Niro has donned a remarkably big nose to better embody Jake La Motta and bears virtually no resemblance to the character he played in "Taxi Driver."

I ignored what *la belle de nuit* said and kissed the hand anyway. "Now, now."

Hm. La Motta is in a room now with a beautiful platinum blonde. Platinum never looked so good as it does on a black-and-white screen. Most everything actually looks better, as though etched out. Perhaps not De Niro with his strange new proboscis. The blonde is too much. Too much for him. He walks over to a dresser on top of which stands a glass jug full of ice water which he pours down his pants.

After the film, Claire and I walked down to Flip's on 19th street and ordered a couple of beers. 1960s hits were playing in the background.

*I'm hungry for your true love baby*
*I'm hungry through and through*

I liked the music. While disco brought my morale down to sub-freezing temperatures, these songs ensnared energy I did not even suspect bubbled inside of me. I liked the old brick structure — with a tiny bit of imagination this could be England. Above all, I liked Claire and her luminous smile. Something so very kissable and caressable about it. But Claire's mouth is not an "it," but rather some creature, some extension alive and pining for tenderness.

And then, her eyes, her inquisitive, intelligent, ironic eyes which seemed as though they wanted to leap out of their sockets. I shall catch them before they hit the ground in a silk or at least cotton handkerchief or, all else failing, use my shirt-tail as a hammock, and ease them back into place. I promise I will not hurt. I will be watchmaker and surgeon general all in one. I will squeeze them ever so delicately and slowly plop them back to the ledge of the orbit, check the eyelids to verify if they are in good flapping condition, and make sure this happens as seldom as possible. I gazed, oblivious to everything else. Strangely, she resembled someone I had known in high school but while I never considered the latter to be attractive, Claire embodied the ideal.

"Your father told me you have lived around the world?"

She seemed embarrassed to hear the question, as if it pained her.

"Well, my sisters and me. We did go to primary school in India and lived off and on in the States and London."

"Nice place. I'd like to go back there."

"Don't I know it. And you spent some time in France, right?"

I watched her fingers as they started playing with a discarded straw.

"Yes. From zero to 18, that is where I lived."

"Long time. I thought you were 100 percent American."

I take a sip from my mug.

"NNN. I think I was expecting the Universal Wire Press to bring me back in some respects to my halcyon high-school days."

"Those good old halcyon days. And then?"

Many of the words she said appeared to hide a second meaning, as though the English language itself were an excuse to make jokes, as though she were living like a critic in some perched booth.

"Then came college and America. First Montana then Maine and Massachusetts."

"Wow. And now UWS. The best of both worlds?"

"In some ways. This marked a return to the motherland, but a different motherland."

"What do you mean by that?"

"UWS is professional France, journalistic France, France of the 1980s, France overseas. What with my working at night and everything... even if I had continued during the day shift, it seems that it would have taken time to break the ice, to become one of the boys, to make friends. Of course, all that is water under the bridge now."

"I would choose another crowd anyway if I were you; most of them are pretty tedious."

"Joffre seems like a nice guy."

"Joffre is great."

"Pétard..."

"... is a pain."

"Mm. It's funny. Some of them, like Petitcolis, even greet me in English. To them, I am the American who by some fluke of nature speaks French. But I do not have or no longer have the looks or the mannerisms."

"Of the old country?"

She understood. She was bilingual, bicultural, and beautiful.

"Exactly. Something does not quite fit. Of course, my father is American and I have not lived in France for four years. I knew France up until the mid-1970s. Things do change."

She nodded. The straw was quite unidentifiable by now.

"Does your father drive an Oldsmobile?"

"No, actually he drives a Renault 15 with the steering wheel on the right. Why do you ask?"

"I don't know; he seemed the Oldsmobile type."

"I'll have to tell him. Personally, I always wanted a Jeep, but my Dad said they were dangerous because they turned over. I might have to settle for a Bug."

"Great car. I learned to drive on one."

Bukowski had one for a while. I told her about Gronket and the rosé incident.

"Rosé? My father always told me rosé was inferior wine."

"I know, my father says the same; but on a hot summer day a good rosé de Provence does hit the spot."

At 2:00 a.m. we asked for the check.

"Come on, let me chip in," she said.

"No, you can pay some other time we go out together."

"Together? That sounds nice."

Claire, my love.

"Do you believe in the theory of compensation?"

"What do you mean?"

"Well, the fact that your father has no hair and you have the most beautiful hair I've ever seen."

She smiled.

Before we parted I gave her a small kiss on the mouth. I closed my eyes and caught a glimpse of the Milky Way. She said my eyes were full of stars. I kissed her a second time. A third was not to follow.

"My mother says I should not step beyond certain limits," she said. "Oh darn, I can't find my keys. I must've left them inside, which means that I will probably have to sleep in the bushes."

\* \* \*

I called her up the next morning. She did not have to sleep in the bushes; her mother was awake and had let her in.

"That's a shame because I was thinking of writing a story for the agency on people who sleep in bushes."

When I'm hot, I'm hot.

She laughed.

"I had a great time last night."

La-la-la-la-la.

\* \* \*

"What a butt-fucked asshole!" Simon, always the stylish one, comments the following weekend as I show him the sites of the capital and tell him how Mouluvert fired me. "I can't believe you're going out with his daughter. That must put him in a tizzy."

"She's the sweetest thing you've ever seen."

"Lose a job, get a woman."

"Too bad I can't have both."

"Yeah."

With Simon around, the city acquires more character. Life resumes. His hair has grown even longer than mine and his clothes recall those Frank Zappa wore 20 years ago.

To flee the cold we hopped from one museum on the Mall to the next and then walked until our throats were revived by an Irish coffee at One Step Down, an old jazz club on Pennsylvania Avenue, not unlike one of the *caves* in Saint-Germain-des-Prés.

"Apparently Pop's doing a little better," Simon said.

A Mingus melody is playing in the back of the room which carries a pleasant scent of old wood and whiskey.

"That's good. I hope he makes it."

We concentrate on the drinks and the smoke rising from them. Our gazes avoid one another. We love the old man, oh how we love him! But there's the other one, the Jekyll, the Dracula, the Führer, the Torquemada who could turn a quiet early evening into a Courtroom of vultures, lawyers, and inquisitors screaming GUILTY! GUILTY! GUILTY! GUILTY! TRAITOR! WHORE! TURD! FAGGOT! COWARD! MORON! — simply because he had seemingly been contradicted or had misinterpreted a compliment, feeling it was lukewarm, or, heard a question that should not have been asked at that particular time. The storm could rage for weeks or peter out in a couple of days. Then silence, then a few words. They used to sound like the first birds chirping in the spring; then, Quentin Nostran the poet would reappear, and pretty soon would return to the garden and tend to his daffodils or dahlias, singing one of his favorite songs.

"Pop's remarkably resilient."

"True."

Huddled up, blowing clouds of steam through our nostrils, we trudged into Georgetown, past the Chesapeake and Ohio Canal. Barely after completion, this romantic means of transportation, running parallel to the Potomac, which is practically unnavigable past the Key Bridge, was superseded by the railroads. The canal is now distinguished by lack of water. How very odd. And somewhat sad.

"Sometimes," I say, "it seems as though the old man had returned to the States because he knew he didn't have that much longer to go. Like those elephants who leave the flock..."

"You wonder how life could continue without him."

"It might be better for Mum."

"You should've seen him when you were gone to college. It was agony. All that yelling... Like the guy was functioning on pure venom. If it wasn't Mum, it was me; if it wasn't me, it was Goblin."

Goblin, the black and white farm cat, more persecuted by Pop than a bourgeois by a Bolshevik.

"But, Simon, look at him now."

"I know. The stroke seems to have done him good."

"So many times I've felt like writing him off and then he comes back, turns on the charm..."

We turn right at Thomas Jefferson Street.

"Shit," Simon mutters, "I thought I'd be escaping some of the cold down here, but it's almost like Syracuse."

"I don't remember Maine or Montana to be a hell of a lot colder. At least it keeps the assholes off the street."

"Assholes favor the heat. Albert, didn't we park somewhere here?"

"Up the street."

"I'm beginning to get my bearings."

"How does Vietnamese food strike you?" I ask as we pass by a bright-red façade. "Is this restaurant any good?" I ask a tall young woman with sexy front teeth and a handsome grey coat about to enter.

"Very nice, I highly recommend it."

So recommendable it is that there are no available tables.

"Why don't you join me?" the woman, with the sexy teeth and as it turns out chestnut hair, suggests. "I'm supposed to meet my sister here."

The sister arrives with her boyfriend, soon to be followed by the spring rolls and the imperial duck. The conversation turns to Peugeot automobiles, which they love, and the revelation of a parking space at a nearby hotel which facilitates matters for the motorist inclined to sojourn in this part of town.

And cinema.

"Would you like to see a film out in Virginia?" Sexy Teeth proposes.

Simon and I look at each other, shrug our shoulders.

"What's playing?"

"*Stir Crazy*, with Gene Wilder and Richard Pryor."

Simon's head tilts to one side.

"Okay."

And down the freeway we rush, following the Peugeot 504 Diesel.

The movie, while no stroke of genius, turns out to be pleasant in its own Hollywood way. When it was finished, we bade the girls goodbye, never to see them again. Washington, city of transience. On the way back to Park Mapletree, Simon tells me:

"I tried to grab the hand of the one with the sexy teeth during the film."

"You dog!"

"And I banged her in the men's room... No actually she turned me down."

I unlock the door to my own love-nest. Davey is watching television.

"I think Mum wanted us to call her," I tell Simon.

In the meantime, Davey switches off the tube and retreats to his room.

"Is he noisy or what?"

"I'm telling you."

The telephone rings 500 miles further north.

"Things are looking bad," says Mum. "Big taxes must be paid on the house, bills are piling up right and left — including your father's medical bill. Physically he has improved, but he is still confused."

"Tsk."

"This calls for permanent medical assistance which means a male nurse will have to stay in the house or removal to a nursing home. Also, alimony must be paid to the ex-wife. All I have to live on is your father's retirement wage, the social security and a quickly diminishing trust fund."

"God."

"And he hasn't written a will, so things are more complicated. We might have to sell the house."

*

## All of the Night

*Cinderella in black*
*You drove me wild*
*Me, the closet prince*
*Aesthetically insane*

*Baby, I'm not weird alone*
*And it cuts ever so deep*
*The dentist's drill is a newborn's dry kiss*
*Compared to the metamorphosis*
*Of Eden to Zilch*

*Alone in the chestnut cream colored vessel*
*On the long, long road*
*Sparkling with angry lights*
*I advert my attention to*
*The radio fuzz.*

Michael Kent

# XIV

# DEEP DOWN

Back at the Zoo. Balthazar is parked down the hill. Rock Creek Park is as bare as a hairless cranium. The sky is overcast; the air is chilly but humid. Ideal weather for jumping off a bridge. I am reminded of a song by Jacques Brel. Claire and I wander from cage to cage. From time to time she skips like a little child.

"You know, in some ways I am happy to be fired and quit the night shift; I am delighted to be leaving my roommate."

"He's a toad."

"That's right, you spoke to him. I just want to take off, go to Europe, Asia, South America, Africa, out west. Wyoming, maybe. We can find work on a ranch. I have a little money saved up... And you can come with me," I tell Claire, clutching her hand.

The hand remains motionless, like dry algae, while her foot inside a desert boot kicks a pebble.

"Honestly. Do you think I can just take off like that? I've got to finish my classes. I can't just leave my parents."

I feel a pair of shears clamp around my throat.

"I understand. But do you think I can stay in this city? I don't want to become just another bureaucrat. I want to move, do things, see the world. But nothing makes sense if you're not around."

I LOVE YOU.

"Now, now."

It is not so much that she is turning me down, although that hurts too, it is how she is doing it. I feel I am in a coal mine, searching for some precious gem but there is nothing there, only coal and the impression that since I am in the mine I should seek further.

"You're my sole reason for staying here."

For being alive.

We walk past the zebra cage. A male is chasing a female. Go, go.

"I cannot accept that kind of responsibility. I feel torn between you and my father and I don't want to be in the middle."

Where art thou, Juliet?

We enter the house of bats. While it is difficult to make most of the animals budge, the bats are in perpetual motion. Can there be no in-between? We walk away from the zoo nurturing our zebra feelings.

*　*　*

My successor has been delayed, so I am staying at the agency an extra couple of weeks. Li-li-li.

*　*　*

Two nights ago, Claire and I decided to go to a drive-in theater. Somewhere in Maryland, east of the city. Funny, you look at a map, see the name of towns, and you, or at least I, imagine a village square, with a church, trees, and a fountain, but all you find are rows of long brick buildings, strings of lights, stores, stores and more stores, with parking lots.

I flip on the radio. We hear the Police, singing "Don't Stand So Close to Me."

"You know Claire, I don't care much for the top-40 these days, but this song is rather nice."

"Uh-huh, quite acceptable. But, could you drive a little more slowly? You're making me awfully nervous."

Women always say that but they don't mean it.

"At least I always put on my turn signal, which is more than you can say for most of the other jerks on the road."

"WATCH OUT!"

"I saw him. Are you sure this is the right road?"

Once again, the Nostran sense of direction or lack thereof coupled with Claire's fuzzy recollection constrained us to make a bit of a detour but we made it to the largest parking area of them all, stopped the car by the post with the speakers, hooked up said-speaker on the window of the car. I felt as though I was in "American Graffiti." I had never been to this kind of place before and my heart was bursting with excitement. Claire was looking better than ever. More woman-like. There she was by my side. O mirth!

We kissed a little but I never was able to get a feel of those two big devils she is hiding under her sweater.

"Be reasonable," she kept on saying.

"But I've been reasonable for God knows how long! I'm only made of flesh and blood."

"Don't give me those tired clichés. Come on, be a good boy."

First the father, then the daughter. I stared at the large screen as kindly tourists were being swallowed up by the sand. Good. If only the real world could do the same, if only with six packs and fast-food packaging. An XXX movie was to follow but Claire insisted we drive away. Too bad, it might have inspired her.

"Please drive slowly… Albert?"

"Okay."

I've plugged in my Rolling Stones tape.

"Let's spend the night together," Claire sings along with it.

"Is this a proposition?"

She smiles enigmatically. The road moves on like a tarantula.

"Tsk, don't be silly. Honestly, what would my parents think?"

"You could come to Park Mapletree…"

"No way! What kind of girl do you take me for anyway? Don't talk like that."

"By the way, Claire, what's the time?"

"You don't have a watch?"

"Obviously not, or I wouldn't ask."

"My, we are in a grumpy mood. 10:45."

It was time I returned to work.

*   *   *

Things go in circles. Suddenly, back at the office, Mouluvert finds my production very acceptable again.

"If you'd worked like this all along," he says, "we never would have had to lay you off."

"Then can you take me back?"

"No, it's too late; the new fellow is on his way."

Thanks for the glimmer of hope, pal.

Joffre: "I overheard Hertzen and Mouluvert talking about your work, and they both seemed very impressed."

Pétard: "I warned you; you wrote too much, you should've kept to a more humble scale. You were writing almost as much as all of the day team combined. No one likes excess zeal; plus, the more you write, the more vulnerable you are, the more you're likely to trip — even though your language skills, your English, is better than anybody else's around here. Of course, you were definitely undertrained. In Paris, they stick with you for three months straight before they let you do anything by yourself; how long was it before you started? Two and half weeks? Minimal supervision... By the way, I met your successor, he's the son of the Luxembourg Prime Minister."

Interesting.

*　　*　　*

A side street in Georgetown. N or Prospect. A little brick dive where you can order sandwiches and beer. A natural place. A hangout for students and bohemian young adults. There she is, sitting at the table, facing me. Wearing black. Taking a dainty sip from her mug. I am a lucky and happy man. My heart is pounding merrily away.

"Claire?"

"Yes Albert?"

"Er... I have something for you?"

"Don't tell me... A diamond necklace."

There is sarcasm in the smile, but a smile it is. Claire's smile.

"Not quite, but you might like it anyway."

I hand over the little package, the content of which I bought as I walked up Wisconsin Avenue a couple of days ago. A misty day, slightly humid. Her hand seizes it and with the other she tears off the gift-wrap, opens the box and pulls out the bracelet. The silver bracelet.

"Oh, Albert, it's lovely. Actually, much nicer than I really deserve."

"Try it on."

She does. I look at her, at her wrist. She is there in front of me. What more can a man really ask for?

*　　*　　*

The following Friday I meet my successor, Antoine-Joseph de Voors de Luxembourg, at the Mouluvert's where he is staying until he finds a place of his own.

"I know a good place," says I, "not too far from the Pentagon. It's a great place, great location, between Washington and Alexandria."

"Old Town?"

"About a mile down the road."

He is wearing a brown jacket and a goatee at the end of his chin. Something in his demeanor, his nervous mannerisms reminds me of *The Wizard of Oz*'s scarecrow.

"Yes, that might interest me. Do you have a telephone number?"

"Why certainly."

Claire, exceptionally, has donned a dress. My goodness such shapely legs; too bad she is also wearing plastic sandals. Better than sneakers, but still quite silly. Perhaps that is Claire. Mr. Luxembourg, sounding like a newspaper article, begins to discuss the economy:

"The number of carmakers is shrinking; only a few of the brands we know today will be around by the year 2000. I think the Chrysler Corporation will probably be the first to go."

"I don't."

"How come?"

"You see Chrysler vehicles everywhere. They manufacture the U.S. army tanks. Psychologically, they're a huge slice of the American Pie, a huge employer. They're not going to give up without a fight. And I think Iacocca is the man to do it."

He moves his lower lip forward.

Claire does not appear interested in the least. She is walking around the room knitting her eyebrows.

"I'm going to the den if anybody cares to join me."

Luxembourg winks at me. So, along with Burnette the dog, I follow.

"Lay off will you, stupid pooch," I tell Burnette as he starts to slobber over my leg.

"Come on; don't talk to my dear puppy like that."

"I have feelings too, remember?"

"Of course I do, silly."

The conversation drags on. A peak here, a tease there. We both sit in wicker chairs facing the black of night and our fuzzy reflections in the glass. This room, like all the others in the house, is spartan. Except for a black-and-white photograph on the wall of Mouluvert holding a magnifying glass over his right eye, thereby enhancing his natural good looks and his resemblance of Jean Genet. There is also a watercolor of two elephants on a tightrope. A charming, naive, endearing juxtaposition of yellows, pinks, and grays.

"Did you do that, Claire?"

"Yes, and my sister took the picture."

"They're nice."

I stare back at Claire's brushstroke. Why can't she talk to me the way she painted?

Mrs. Mouluvert brings us some apple juice. I feel as though I have been catapulted back to a country she never seems to have left. Apple juice: right color, wrong flavor, wrong effect. In a couple of seconds there is only a diminishing ice cube at the bottom of my glass. Claire seems plunged in shallow thought; suddenly, she and I do not have much to talk about. It is a signal, time has come to get physical. I take her hand. She withdraws it impatiently. I look at her left wrist, then at the right. She is not wearing the bracelet. My mood shifts from bad to worse.

"You can take my pinky if you like," she says, with a big smile and her eyes pop out. *My pinky*? Gogol was right, women are the devil.

"That's okay."

Meanwhile arpeggios from Rachmaninoff's First Piano Concerto are swelling in the next room where the adults are. Discussing world affairs, as I want to do with Claire, but Claire prefers to play with Burnette, the drooler.

"This kind of music bores me," she says. She is restless.

"Not me."

"Ah, men are all the same, all they can think about is one thing."

"Politics?"

"No, you know what I'm referring to."

I try to capture her gaze. No success.

"I think it's time for me to leave."

The chair creaks as I get up.

"Come on, don't be a snob," she says.

"There's just so much I can take."

I walk towards the door, open it.

"Come on, stay a little bit."

"Why don't you come to me?"

She slams the door. Screw you too! Screw you good! I bid the adults goodbye and walk to Balthazar, start the engine and take off at full speed, whizzing in and out of the Massachusetts Avenue traffic, paying little heed to the lines on the pavement or the color of the lights. Let's see how fast this monster can really go.

Claire, Claire! Why even give me hope? Why play with me? Why wear a pretty dress and ruin it with plastic sandals? I need affection, I need love and I'm horny, God damn it! Oh, and by the way, coinciding with Reagan's inauguration, the 52 hostages have just been released; so, deep down I am very happy.

# Part II

# XV

# LA GROSSE POMME
# & OTHER BITES

G ood to be back in New York, breathe the electric air, walk up
the bustling avenues, plow my way through the crowd, look
up at the summit of skyscrapers, see a full spectrum of humanity:
white collars, blue collars, leave rinky-dink Washington behind; I
even like the smells up here — less sulfuric. There is more to life than
neatly trimmed lawns and neo-classical façades! This is a volcano,
a stampede, a tidal wave, an earthquake; and, when it comes to
buildings, New York offers a variety, a wealth, difficult to find in the
capital. Joffre was right. Good old Joffre, one of the best reporters in
the agency; good old Joffre who could not understand why I had been
fired. It is also pleasant to be a diurnal, a full-fledged day-person; it
is the bare minimum. One needs the photosynthesis, the vitamin D
which the sun provides.

I took the train up to Pennsylvania station and have just gone to see a Mr. Ballsworth at Crawfish-Swill, the prestigious publishing company on Madison Avenue that Pierre Legris, the Universal Wire Press's local correspondent, has enabled me to contact.

To become an editorial assistant, as opposed to what UWS refers to as a "sub-editor." Does this sound like a promotion, or what? For the first time in months I have worn the handsome corduroy suit that my father bought me when we first moved to Stone Harbor. Mouluvert wrote a succinct but fairly complimentary letter of recommendation, talking about my good command of the French language and throwing Spanish in for good measure.

Semi-bald but amply side-burned Archibald Ballsworth informs me, peering in my direction with pale blue eyes through bifocals, that the nature of the job is to push a cart around. I beg your pardon? But not any old cart: a cart full of important and semi-important documents and, well, er, yeah, because, however, then, in order to assist the editors. Those who are using their brains, rather than their feet and legs.

"It's quite exciting at times."

He gives me a connoisseur wink.

"Sure sounds like it."

I was about to ask him if he had ever considered doing commercials for British ale but I figured I shall have plenty of time in the future.

Aside from announcing that his wife is French and that she is great in bed as a result, he did not add much, but the sly devil knows that it is by pushing a cart around that you slowly but surely get to the top.

"One day you may push the biggest cart in the company."

That is why one goes to a good college.

"Sounds ducky," I respond enthusiastically to add a little drama.

"We'll keep you in mind."

I give him a hearty handshake. A hug would be too effusive. Even though I am quite tempted. I save it instead for Ferdinand Latulipe, the mad poet from the Bronx who has come down to the island of Manhattan to greet me. His blonde hair has gotten longer but he is the same rosy-cheeked, bearded lad I knew in Maine. A leprechaun in the big city.

We talk about jobs, my father, his, the Capital City.

"One things that bothers me, Ferdinand, about Washington, is the way the place is so compartmentalized. It's like, Georgetown, blam, the historic district; K Street, blam, the business district; then, blam, a residential area; then a huge forest..."

"That sounds nice."

"It does, except that you feel culture shock at every corner. It doesn't seem to fit together. I don't know... Too many parking lots, too many office buildings. It's not organic."

"A lot of American cities are that way," he says in a ponderous tone. "At least Washington still has a lot of residents. In a lot of cities the people have fled to the suburbs."

"Doesn't exactly stir the blood."

Michael Kent

The words I speak here seem to bear more weight than in other locations I have recently frequented. New York hums with karma; matters count. Conversation is important. It seems that there is always an audience even if nobody is listening.

«*Et les femmes*[13]?» he asks.

I tell him about Claire. Her moods which shoot up and down like Massachusetts Avenue.

"She sounds dangerous."

"I think you might be right. But it's like I'm addicted... She does have a lot of qualities. You should see her."

He shakes his head. Women to him switch from Madonnas to sluts. There is no in-between. He remains distant to preserve the illusion. The subject is making him suddenly uncomfortable.

"Have you been to the Dakota lately?" I ask.

"I'd rather stay away from that whole part of town these days."

"I can see that. Maybe in a couple of years..."

"It bodes badly for times to come."

"Yeah."

The *yeah* of disgust and despair.

I stare up at a gargoyle. New York is full of them.

"Oh, incidentally," says Latulipe, with a grin, "I've got two tickets for a show."

"You devil!"

We enter the big Broadway theater off 52nd Street. Life resumes. If I become an editorial assistant I can forget about America's administrative capital and come up here, push carts and watch plays and drink sangria and eat filet mignon with my old college pal. I shall be closer to Mum and Pop. And Pop, like the Chrysler Corporation, seems to be emerging from the dead. No one can believe it, but not a day goes by without some improvement. First the body; then the mind, at an escargot's pace — but why rush? And no temper tantrums on the horizon.

Before I left the District of Columbia, Claire called me up to say she was sorry. What a woman. I think she would be happy in New York also.

\* \* \*

13  -How about women?

Michael Kent

## THREE POSTCARDS TO CLAIRE

*(Two chained monkeys gaze through a window at the sea. It is a Brueghel reproduction)*

<u>Rangoon</u> *(Where Claire was born)*

I tossed my umbrella in the rain
And naturally
I got wet

But suppose
The clouds had dried out
At that precise moment?

<u>(La Gare Saint-Lazarre, par Claude Monet)</u>

PARIS — *(in French)* Since we have arrived it has not stopped raining. All else having failed we shall attempt to rid ourselves of our umbrellas.

*(A nineteenth century photograph, showing a stage-coach crossing the desert)*

<u>Marrakesh</u> — *(in German)* The sun is shining to such an extent that we have forgotten the very meaning of an umbrella. Tomorrow we are heading to Casablanca.

\*

# XVI

# NEW SURROUNDINGS

B ut this boy will not be pushing a cart around. Pity, I could already picture myself running along the East River, past the vast vaults and soot of the Brooklyn, Manhattan, and Williamsburg Bridges, past the United Nations and Sutton Place, rushing through the traffic and the elements of a consumer's society few like to evoke, brown smoke and little pebbles blowing in my face, gleefully coughing, skillfully avoiding the pot-holes, pushing the cart with Claire wedged inside of it, her knees forming the shape of leggy pyramids, her heels touching her shapely derrière, her delicate lips pressing against a bottle of Clos-Vougeot 1975 offered by Mouluvert senior as a token of affection.

"Have fun, kids! And lucky you, with a cart, you can drink and drive!"

"Now, your turn," I would yell out of breath to my inebriated queen. Instead:

"It was a close call between you and the other fellow, but he had more experience so we finally opted for him," Ballsworth tells me this morning over the phone. This morning after a good night's sleep, rather than a hard, dismal, lonely night at the office. Another feather to grace my failure hat. My ears are beginning to disappear. Chalk it up to experience.

\* \* \*

As I was walking back from a shopping spree over the freeway overpass, I could not help but notice, delicately knotted to the railing, gently fluttering in the February breeze, a little yellow ribbon.

And like Proust after his teeth had locked into the Madeleine, the sight sent me spinning, reeling, howling through the past; once again my heart bled as it had during the last trillion days, the last trillion days of captivity of the poor 52 hostages.

For yes! Never had any country or any people known so violent, so dreadful a humiliation! The victims of the Spanish Inquisition, those who fell, trampled under the Bolshevik boot, the six million Jews, Gypsies, Resistance, politically incorrect — gassed in the concentration camps... all that blood and torture paled in light of what OUR 52 heroic countrymen endured.

And although the media that we enjoy in this unique nation perhaps at times downplayed the ordeal — after all, the U.S.A. is not one of those filthy under-developed nations that relishes in scandal sheets — the American people, perceptive today as they have infallibly been in the past, understood what their duty was: tie a little yellow ribbon all over the place.

Like the knights returning from the Crusades — and was this not a crusade of sorts? — we cherished our heroes as they paraded through our cities. In what some refer to as an inglorious age, we grasped the significance of an unprecedented event. In front of our eyes the Saints were marching in, 52 men, each one bigger and bolder than the next. Alexander the Great, Julius Caesar, Charlemagne, Roland, El Cid, Tannhauser, King Arthur and Sir Lancelot had returned to these better shores, where the salt is saltier and the water, wetter, glittering in their army parkas, as their peers had in armor and gold. And that, we understood.

It is a little difficult at this point to narrate the feats of the 52 martyrs and perhaps not the right time to do so. But it warms the heart and the soul to realize that what one miserable individual, whose name I shall not mention here, labeled the land of Coca-Cola, which might sound nice but could imply that America is overly commercial, that this land has been gouged of a soul. We have stopped detractors in their steps: Americans are not zombies with little transmitters in their heads that certain forces can turn on and off.

(I have to bandage my face now because while I was looking at the yellow ribbon, I tripped over the body of some lazy bum wrapped in an army blanket. I bet he does not even like the army).

\*    \*    \*

Thanks to the pair of scissors with the black rubber coating, the asymmetric circles in which one is supposed to insert one's fingers, purchased virtually four years ago at Big Sky University in the bonnie state of Montana where I spent the overwhelming majority of my freshman year[14], I have cut out a most promising classified advertisement (even though it does not quite suit my ideal), requesting the services of a travel agent. Do I not speak several languages, a couple of which fluently? Are my fingers not used to typing little green letters? Anyhow, does this line of work require a Ph.D.? I called the travel agency. The man at the other end sounded both telephonic and enthusiastic. Of course, this is America where the local religion stipulates you be enthusiastic; still, it never fails to warm the hopeful heart.

The only problem is that we agreed to meet at 9:00 a.m., and to reach Bethesda, wherein the agency lies, I cannot perceive of any other means than to cut through Washington and thus roar down highway 395, which is H.O.V. positive during the rush hour; or, to the readers from former centuries, requires High Occupancy Vehicles, three passengers or more. But, I have an idea. Goodbye Davey Gronkett and down the hill in big Balthazar. There is the bus stop. A dozen people are biding their time and/or reading the newspaper. I park in front of them.

"Anyone interested in getting a quick ride into town?"

They look at one another. Curiosity is getting the better of them. Hm, not a bad car. This might beat waiting in the cold and then having to transfer at the Pentagon. One man says "sure," a bold-headed woman follows suit, and pretty soon, five merry and entrepreneurial people are cruising down 395, which I have recently discovered also bears the name of Shirley. America, land of poetry.

\*　　\*　　\*

Returned I have to George Washington University's housing service. My eyes scan the board. I cannot make the same mistake twice. First of all, avoid Virginia. Especially Park Mapletree. Avoid the suburbs. Concentrate on the District, return where some semblance

---

14   -See THE BIG JIGGETY, the author's first novel.

of life remains. Then I see two names, a couple: Carl and Flora. It has a nice ring to it. My romantic heart swells. I can already picture a thatched roof and lacy curtains. Although in Washington, it is less expensive than my Virginian dwelling. I jot down the telephone number and call them up.

"It's really pleasant up here, a lot of trees, a block from Rock Creek Park, a shopping area nearby," Flora says. Nice voice. "It reminds me of one of those attractive towns in central New York."

Did she say central New York? On an early spring-like day, though winter still looms over the calendar, I drive Balthazar from my distant suburb all the way up Connecticut Avenue's 220 blocks, turn right on Nebraska then left on Utah and end up on 31st Street in front of the tiniest house on the block. Tiny, no thatched roof but solid-looking.

Flora opens the door. She is a smiling, petulant, pretty, mid-size woman with medium-length brown hair. Carl, her live-in boy-friend, is about my height, wears thicker glasses, has black hair and grunts, as guys are supposed to, so I figure he isn't gay. Already a good sign. He disappears with a distraught look into the basement.

"Don't worry about him," Flora says, flashing her impeccable teeth. "He's a Marxist."

"I was going to say!"

Only a Marxist would grunt that way.

I follow Flora up a narrow flight of steps where she shows me a little room with a pleasant view overlooking the street and a door that opens up onto stairs leading to the attic. I like the door, I like the attic; it spells mystery. A fellow with wild black frizzy hair is still living there but will be moving out in a couple of weeks. He looks like he belongs in a rock group but in fact studies geology. We shake hands. He seems as though he is made of rubber and that if I pull hard enough I can wrap his arm around his body a half-dozen times.

"In the meantime," says Flora, "I thought you could live in the basement."

"Mm."

"Would you like to see it?"

"Sure."

I follow down a narrow flight of steps. There it is, the basement. Featuring handsome panels which bear an uncanny resemblance to wood (and are far easier to wash), it comes equipped, at virtually no extra charge, with every possible modern commodity: stove, refrigerator, washing machine, and dryer. No television or stereo, but why be gluttonous? All these appliances, which Flora seems to have kept thus far dust-free, stand within walking if not touching distance of one another and the bedroom, where I plan to invite future conquest(s). Time and skill permitting. We return upstairs.

"Nice car! Is that yours?" Flora asks looking out the dining-room window at Balthazar.

"It's been in the family since 1964."

"Looks like it's in pretty good shape," Carl adds. He speaks! The Kremlin is becoming translucent. I am about to leave when a question of utmost importance dawns on me.

"By the way..."

"Yes?"

"Yeah?"

"Do y'all have an insinkerator?"

Carl and Flora look at one another, then at me.

"We sure do."

"That's good to know."

I think that, as they were concerned, it was the car which convinced them to have me share their love nest. Nice aesthetics and good collateral. I drive back to Northern Virginia singing a song by the Kinks.

> *I'm not content to be with you in the daytime*
> *Girl I want to be with you all of the time*
> *The only time I feel alright is by your side*
> *Girl I want to be with you all of the time*

My mother never believes that things change. *"Plus ça change, plus c'est la même chose[15]*," she says, yet Luxembourg has moved away from the Mouluverts and into the Mapletree duplex to enjoy Davey, Davey Gronket, green television, and I-395. And I have moved out, taking all my belongings, including my handsome marble table. I managed to sell the bed to Lux for a profit. Perhaps that is my vocation: business.

---

15  -The more things change, the more they remain the same.

Michael Kent

As for my new if temporary residence: the basement, I have discovered one disadvantage: the switch for the lights in the sleeping quarters is very far removed from my (double) bed; so, when I want to go to sleep, I have to get up again, turn off the lights and then fumble my way through darkness. Impractical.

Tonight, I opted for the bold approach: I thought I would try to beat the light — impossible, but worth a try. Alas! Like trying to get a dog to wear eyeglasses, I did not quite succeed. Instead I failed miserably and bumped into the refrigerator.

DARN!

It is very frustrating not to be as fast as a silly light. Or, for that matter, to get the canine species to appreciate myopia, hypermetropia, presbyopia, astigmatism or Duane Syndrome — most of which I suffer from to one degree or another.

I think I will get into my big muscle car and drive away to Wyoming. With or without Claire. I am getting sick of basements inside tiny houses. Give me air! Give me big skies! Montana, where art thou?

\* \* \*

The travel specialists in Bethesda, off East-West Highway, felt I lacked experience. Back to The Washington Post and its classifieds, depressed at the number of options opened to me. Where does one start? Who? Where? Why? When? The four *W*s never felt so double-u-ish. Should I get into advertising? And sell my soul to the Mephistopheles of Madison Avenue? Bookkeeping? It has a literary ring to it. Clerk for an adult bookstore? But I would have to wear a gas mask and plastic gloves. Plus, I just turned down a part-time position at a "respectable" bookstore because the pay was too low. Graphic Arts? That's more like it. Photography? Fierce competition, even though that was my best subject in college. Editing? Yes, but, and. Go-go dancing? Good exercise, wrong sex. Girl Friday? I feel as though I am on an overpopulated desert island. Too many footprints to decipher on sand which the ocean no longer laps.

Borrowing Carl's typewriter and sitting down at his desk in the office next to my bedroom-to-be, I write a few letters, typing up a new résumé each time since there is no photocopying service in the neighborhood, except for the library which charges an exorbitant 15 cents.

I make a few phone calls. *No! We need someone with more experience... That will not do... The position has been filled... Try again in six months... That was a mistake...*

Suddenly a friendly voice, light in the mine, hope at the end of the long dark tunnel. It is a man at Time-Life, he needs someone to sell books over the telephone. Business + literature, what could go wrong? I click my heels, jump into the car and drive over to Wisconsin Avenue, a mere ten blocks away, for an interview.

\*

# XVII

# TIME OF LIFE

"What would you say best describes you?" Darwell asks me. He is a little black man in a silk white shirt split down the middle by a navy blue necktie.

"I don't know..."

Jeeze. What kind of question is that?

I look at him, he looks at me.

"My creativity, my sensitivity..."

He scratches his goatee, stares at me intently. This is not any old job interview.

"Okay," he continues in a raspy voice, "now that you are a Time-Life contract employee, I want you to channel all that creativity, all that sensitivity into selling our books over the phone."

I look back at him, feeling as though I have never attended Burdon College. I should not have signed that contract with my blood.

"Yes, Darwell."

"Come, let me show you the phone room."

We leave the small office for a large brightly lit room full of people dialing numbers, conversing enthusiastically about the newest collections the company has to offer. Most are sitting, but some stand or rather dance, moving their legs from time to time. Once in a while: "gling!" a bell goes off, while a man by a blackboard that everyone faces jots down the number of sales corresponding to a list of names.

"Now, Al — do you like Al or Albert?"

"Al is fine."

"Al, I will give you a sound-proof booth where you can use our Watts-line to dial customers in a given area of the country. I'll provide you with a list. Several lists. These are people who've purchased books from our collections before and are likely to buy more. Do you follow me?"

"Loud and clear, Darwell."

"Great. I like your spirit and the spirit is what keeps this thing moving."

I like your spirit too. Actually, your necktie is not bad.

"Each and every one of these booths contains our rap sheet with the basic questions that will move the customer in a certain direction, which will make it very hard for *he* or *she* to actually say no."

"That's brilliant."

Even though your grammar is incorrect. I purse my lips.

"We try. The sheet indicates how to counter any type of negative answer. Some very astute people have researched this."

"Impressive."

"You're right. As you can see, it's always very important to say: "I understand;" BUT, do you know you can cancel at any time after a 10-day trial period. There are a number of other come-backs; a good sales rep can sell anything. Anything. It's a question of technique and experience. Some people here make very big money. Basic pay plus commission, not to mention the prizes and the stimulating atmosphere. So Al, I want you to pick up one of those phones and show me what you're made of."

"Okay, Darwell, but I'm a little nervous."

A thin smile appears on his lips.

"We all are at the beginning, it's part of the game."

*All in the wonderful game that we know as love.*

I dial a number in Urbana, Illinois.

"Hello, Mrs. Cruxley, my name is Al Nostran. Mrs. Cruxley, I believe you purchased the Time-Life Western series. We were interested to know how you like them."

"Oh, ah, my husband and I enjoyed them very much."

"Well, that's great because we have now come up with the aviation series, a beautiful, leather-bound collection where you can read about Eddie Rickenbacker, the German Red Baron... You can start today for only $10.99 a volume."

"Aviation? My husband used to fly!"

"There you go... So shall I put you down?"

"Sure, that would be great."

Darwell turns to me, grabs my shoulder.

"Alright Al! That's a sale, but don't forget to ring the bell when a customer accepts."

I see a little breast-shaped ring — the hotel concierge type bell — on the table in front of me. I try it. Gliiing.

"Do I hear a sale?" says the man at the blackboard.

"No Pete," says Darwell, "it's Al trying it out."

"But won't the customer feel manipulated?" I ask. "It's like I caught a fish or something. It's like saying, 'hey sucker,' gotcha."

Darwell gives me a peculiar look.

"Don't worry about that, just keep the sales moving. So far you're doing great."

Darwell walks away. I am alone now. The walls are painted a bright, happy, yellow; sun streams in from Wisconsin Avenue.

Not all customers turn out to be as understanding as Mrs. Cruxley and during the confirmation phone call she canceled. It is a sad day when someone with such a sweet voice cannot be trusted. Some of the sales people, my colleagues, somehow manage to sell 10 books per hour. America is not running out of readers. Or book buyers at least. While I am not at the bottom of the line I never seem to make any commission.

As the days drift by, I did however land a whole slew of gifts including a shower curtain, a portable telephone, two books on poultry cooking (actually the same one multiplied by two), two more on collectibles, three on World War II.

"Albert?!" Darwell calls out after my first week.

"Yes?"

He walks up to me. The temperature outside has dipped so he is wearing a cardigan. And a frown that would make a young child cry.

"Did I just hear you hang up on a customer?"

Big Darwell has tapped the lines.

"He started it. He was becoming insulting. I don't have to deal with that."

"Al; rule number 1: never hang up on a customer."

"Even if he's rude?"

The little fellow inside of me is cracking.

"Yes. It's not professional. I'll call him back myself and apologize."

"Thanks."

There is a man I count on when times get rough.

I dialed and I dialed and I dialed. The red telephone's earpiece collecting wax and grease in the process. I would bring a handkerchief to work and wipe it. And then, what a shine! Perhaps I should market this instead of books, this is something people really do need. Ears will continue to grease up long after the last book has been shelved. With some customers, I found that singing helped. Especially midwestern women.

"Helloooo, this is Albert Nostran calling uuuuuuuuuuup, from Waaaaaaaaaaaaaaaashshshshshsingtooooooooooooooooooooooonnnnn. AAAAAAAAAnd hoooooooooooooowww diiiiiiid yoooooooooooou enjoy our cooking series?"

"They were fine but I don't want anymore. My husband just lost his job and..."

"I understand. Goodbye."

"Albert?"

"Yes Darwell?"

"I overheard your conversation."

Again?

"Yes?"

"You should've insisted."

"But if her poor husband just lost his job?"

"Tell her we have financing plans that can help."

"Weeeeeee haaaaaaave fiiinancing, yes financing, available for only youu."

Michigan: "That sounds good."

"You bet yer high-heeled boots."

South Dakota: "I'm interested."

"Put it there, pal."

New Hampshire: "Are you a recording?"

"No, I'm flesh and blood and..."

Click.

California: "Oh, and another thing."

"Sure. Time-Life is always listening."

"Fuck you."

Delaware: "There was an article in Time I did not agree with the other day."

Like a sales rep is going to answer editorial questions? Get real, man.

"Sorry, sir, that's not my department, but if you try our toll-free number, they'll be ready to help you."

"You merry prankster. Say hi to the señora."

The coast people proved more difficult. South was good; Midwest, as the song goes, was the best. Teenagers were as good or better. Like a knife cutting into butter at room temperature. Every possible item to them sounded awesome, fascinating. No wonder corporate America has zoomed in on them. Their formative, impulsive years coupled with an educational system which teaches them more to accept than to question makes them ideal targets. Life has also yet to reach out and touch them with its long, corrupting fingernails.

A couple of times I called my brother, adrift in the Syracusian marasma and snow.

"I don't know what it is with these women up here, I'm not getting anywhere."

"How about coming down soon?"

"Sure. How does next weekend strike you?"

"Perfect. I've got to work one day but we'll figure something out."

I also called my mother. Pop is coming along, adapting to Del Cove, the nursing home.

"Del Cove?" I say. "It sounds like something out in California."

"Oh, you know how they try to be cute..."

"Don't I. What's it like?"

"Not bad, as far as those places go. The nurses seem a bit more reverent than in Salem. There are actually a couple of male nurses who are extremely devoted. Also, it's in Stone harbor, up the street, so that's more convenient for me to drive or even walk there. They organize these activities in which the patients are supposed to participate. Once a week a piano player performs on this upright piano in the dining hall area. I mean, how corny can you get? This country never ceases to amaze me. I suppose it's nice though in a way. Needless to say, your father refuses to join the group while all the others are giddily clapping and singing along. I think that already says something."

I smile.

"And how is he doing?"

"He's in a wheelchair most of the time, with a catheter; he's lost a lot of weight — no wonder with the kind of food they give him there. The other day, I saw him in some awful polyester thing he would never dream of wearing normally, while his roommate had *his* nice tweed jacket; still, he is extremely sweet and his health is improving — to such an extent, the doctor says that he might return home."

But what if he reverts to his old nasty self? Mum is concerned and I am concerned for her. However, she has hired Maître William Winston, my fellow alumnus lawyer in Gloucester, to investigate, and certain thorny issues are being tackled; a little more money is trickling in. Perhaps she will not have to sell the new house.

"Albert?" Darwell's voice resonates.

"Yes?"

"I haven't heard a sale from you in over an hour."

"This is the calm before the storm, Darwell."

"I'm counting on you."

The Time-Life hours are not bad: noon to four, Monday through Saturday. I park old Balt in the parking lot of the bank across the street. My bank. So far no tickets — which is not bad in a city that derives half its revenue from the little pink slips that do not deteriorate in the rain. This particular neighborhood, Friendship Heights, is more civilized. Although the general architecture cannot be retraced to any particularly noble era.

Driving back to Carl and Flora's I have discovered the joys of National Public Radio, the classical music and their news program "All Things Considered," preceded by the equally excellent "Monitor Radio." But, the latter only starts at 4:30. I am swinging my hand to the sounds of a Mendelssohn symphony when a flash breaks the air: *"Ronald Reagan has been shot outside the Capital Hilton. He has been rushed to George Washington University Hospital."*

And this man is against gun control. "Makes it safe for the criminals. Runs against the Constitution." Funny how the pro-gun people become so emotional about the Constitution when it touches that particular amendment and not the others. I remember the story I wrote for UWS about his wife, Nancy, and how she keeps a little golden hand gun by the side of her bed. Probably if old Ronnie tries some monkey business.

"Honey, I'm in the mood tonight."

"Oh yeah? Well take that!" POW-POW-POW. Suddenly a dreaded thought distorts my features. Where was Nancy in all this? Working out at the gym, or...? Or...?

The radio has not returned to Mendelssohn and I find out that it is one John Hinckley (Junior) who pulled the trigger. The reason is obvious: he had seen "Taxi Driver" and wanted to impress Jody Foster, who plays the pre-adolescent prostitute in that movie.

I park the car in front of the new house, turn off the engine, but continue to listen to the radio. The president is pulling through, and his press secretary Nicholas Brady might end up in a wheelchair. My mind reverts to John Lennon who was not even granted second-best.

\* \* \*

*I could never understand why I had killed him in the first place, and my mind is rather unclear as to when I did it, yet like all murderers I had to return to the scene of the crime.*

*The sky was still light as I walked towards the beaten-down garage where my mother used to park her little VW — next to another shed I had nicknamed "the prison" (and where I had placed many rusted objects). I stared up at the naked beams which had probably once supported another floor, but all that could be seen now was the inside of the roof.*

*Then it got dark. Either I relived the scene or this was a new occurrence running parallel to the first and somehow attempting to eclipse it. Lennon was dead; his neck had been partly severed and blood almost pink in hue kept gushing out, like liquefied strawberry jam. Everything then turned red.*

*Me or someone else proceeded to tie the ex-Beatle's corpse to Paul McCartney's, who kept on insisting that <u>he</u> was alive. He was badly shaven; but, still, that was no excuse to tie him up. Another Lennon smiled from below while the two bodies were still being tied. I became a mere spectator.*

*The two bodies were then shoved inside a potato sack which was hoisted up into the attic.*

\* \* \*

Snow is descending, like talcum powder on a baby's bottom, gently covering everything on the ground below, adapting to the most crooked shapes, from dead branches to fire hydrants, wrought-iron banisters to slated roofs, individual air-conditioning units to parking meters, automobiles to discarded beer cans. Snow, the great equalizer, and suddenly everything looks beautiful. A Glinka passage drifts through my head.

And no buses on Connecticut Avenue, where the Cleveland Park Metro Station is due to open sometime in the 25th century. *In the year 2525...* I am wearing my shiny green aviator jacket with the orange lining and my Finnish hat with the flaps down like a Soviet guard at the Chinese border. But I am very sober and not getting any warmer. I never realized my nose was so long. Maybe it extends when the temperature plunges. Other people are waiting too, looking like mannequins in a store window. Cars are crawling at an escargot's pace. My stomach feels empty.

The light turns red. A woman with a new perm is at the wheel of the first car in line. She is looking onward as though she has no peripheral vision. I knock on the frosted window of the second one. A black man with glasses and impressive sideburns opens the door.

"Come on in, buddy."

"Thanks."

The radio is turned to a news program. "Today, an Air Florida jet, minutes after take-off, crashed into the 14th Street Bridge; there seem to be no survivors."

"Holy mackerel!" I exclaim.

"There's also been a collision down in the Metro, for the first time since the system started," the driver informs me. "Man, look at this weather..."

I can feel my Nordic cheekbones swelling. Suddenly, I am on a sleigh, cracking my whip at the dogs, headed for the South Pole, picturing my former colleagues at the Universal Wire Service typing feverishly away, staring at their two fingers as the Video Display Terminal fills with little green bugs.

*     *     *

"I am sick," I tell Darwell. In the background I hear bells ring, cries of enthusiasm. "I'll make it in on Monday."

"Okay, take care," a somber voice responds. Does he suspect something?

The day is overcast, a little snow remains on the ground, but Simon bursts out laughing. Simon whom I have just picked up at National Airport. Simon looking quite hirsute.

"Oh, you should've heard yourself: 'Hi! I'm sick!' Like you're ready to arm wrestle a bull."

"Did I? Well it's a crappy job anyhow. No future. I've probably told you this before, but I did like UWS."

"Except that it sounds like they boned you up the ass."

"No wonder heterosexuality is a dying phenomenon."

We go downstairs to the kitchen. Carl and Flora are at their respective and respectable jobs. A little yellow *post-it* note is dangling from one of the pans. I turn to Simon, "Let's see what it says."

*"Clean me better, next time."*

The image of a gloating Davey Gronket appears in front of me. Why do you never use detergent? It pollutes. You should use it. Aaaaaah my ulcer is bursting. Let me get an umbrella.

"Pretty petty stuff," Simon comments.

"I'll say. But they are in general, better people, more enlightened, more intelligent than Gronket. You know he complained about the fact that the heat bill had gone up when you stayed there?"

"I'm not surprised. He kept on asking me, when are you leaving?"

I shake my head, open the refrigerator, pull out a pack of whole wheat bread, a can of corn, some mayonnaise, and prepare the sandwich I have invented.

"It's a little on the heavy side but pretty good," says Simon, after a couple of bites.

"I live on this stuff."

Then I open a plastic bag of frozen fries which I dump into a pan of oil. A cloud of hissing smoke billows up to the ceiling. My brother munches on the corn-mayo-wheat looking most introspective. The potatoes sizzle, turn part golden, part black. I serve them.

"I wonder how many calories we're putting away in this, er, meal," Simon says.

"Not to worry, you're not fat and neither am I. Plus, there's no meat..."

"True. Do you have any orange juice?"

"Sure, help yourself."

He walks over to the refrigerator with a most purposeful look on his face, opens the door, grabs the juice container, shakes it up in what I find to be an obscene manner, and pours half of it down his gullet. It used to be Coca Cola; since College he has become more health conscious.

"Any mayonnaise on the fries?" I ask.

Americans favor ketchup, the French like mustard, but the Belgians, ah the Belgians, but the Belgians, prefer mayonnaise. *Une fois*[16], as they say.

"A little."

We are sitting in Flora's dining room, which is big enough for a table around which four people can sit.

"Aren't you going to finish your fries?" I say.

If my father taught me anything, it is to empty my plate.

"They're cold on the inside."

His eyes seem a little sad, his voice mournful.

"So what? It's wasteful. Eat."

"Okay."

"You know, one day, eating fries which are still frozen on the inside might become a delicacy."

My brother lights up a cigarette and blows smoke at the ceiling.

"Would you be interested in seeing the National Arboretum?" I ask him.

"Absolutely. But promise me one thing."

"What's that?'

"That we'll dine in a restaurant tonight."

"One day I'll cook so well you'll be chewing the plate to savor the last drop of sauce."

"I have no doubt about it."

Rather than contradict on the most superficial level, my brother has refined the art of diplomatic and imaginative sarcasm.

And off to the arboretum, in Balthazar. An island of greenery beyond rows of car dealers and fast-food joints.

\*

16  -One time, methinks a literal translation from "ein Mahl," with which the Germans punctuate their sentences.

# XVIII

# UNDER THE SUN, THE MOON, AND THE STARS

S imon has come and gone and now is flying back to the land of the north whence Canadian winds fiercely blow; but, the sun in the capital of the United States of America is out almost every day and I, like a lizard, am savoring every minute of it. Or every drop, if Phoebus were to be compared to dishwashing detergent. I have quit the job at Time-Life, staying there a total of four weeks which is more than average if I am to believe what people tell me. It seems as though everyone I meet has worked for the organization at one point on another. Time to get my life in gear and enjoy old Phoebus.

Every day, weather permitting — and usually it does — I drive down to Georgetown, park my car in the secret hiding place near the Chesapeake and Ohio Canal. I look at the water. Gone is the winter drought. A family of ducks swims by.

I then sit down on a bench and read. *Crime and Punishment.* Translated by Sidney Monas. The world around me ceases to exist. My father said: "You have to try the Russians: Gogol, Goncharov, Tolstoy, Turgenev, Pushkin, Chekhov. Dostoyevsky is particularly good." Simon and Mum followed the advice, and so am I, living nowadays through Porfiry Petrovich's inquiry into a particularly senseless murder, the anti-bourgeois philosophizing of Andrei Semyonovich Lebezyatnikov, the balancing influence of Sonya Semyovna, and the Nietzschean ravings of Rodion Romanovich Raskolnikov, experiencing the epileptic portrayal as I have rarely experienced anything before. I feel spasms shoot around my body, keep my mouth open lest I bite my tongue off.

"Who's that man shaking on the path, George?" a slightly overweight woman with no chin asks her husband.

Michael Kent

"Oh, just a man reading Dostoyevsky."

The man has enough chin for both of them and sports a pale blue jacket.

"Let's get something to eat."

Now and then, between chapters, I look up and around and stare, in a daze, at the water gushing out of a missing square panel in the lock in front of me, its reflections dancing on the stone under the 30th Street Bridge. The smell of silt carried by a gentle breeze invades my nostrils. On the other bank, in a most geometric work of brick full of angles and balconies, shops await, in particular an art gallery. An outdoor café would be more appropriate, so that I may indulge in a cup of coffee or tea. All this under the celestial orb. I picture the canals of old Saint Petersburg to be quite different.

I do not care much for Georgetown past eight p.m., especially weekend nights when it just turns in to a place to get drunk on cheap beer and pick up women with whom I do not have a chance in the short run, and who probably would not have a chance with me in the long run. Wisconsin Avenue and M Street, although cluttered with people, have the silliest narrowest sidewalks in town; K Street, which is a ghost-town at night, has intelligent and broad sidewalks.

Part of Georgetown's problem resides in the lack of Metro. How much sense a station would make here! Yet the people turned it down. The people! How democratic and yet how plutocratic! "The people" refers in this case to the narrow-minded, provincial bourgeoisie that inhabits the neighborhood. Or inhabited it when the decision was made. They did not want the riff-raff, but the riff-raff will always come. In cars, on motorcycles, bikes, roller skates, skateboards. The Metro cameras would have provided an excellent way to monitor them!

According to certain rumors the terrain was not appropriate, a different geological stratum. But, since when has even the hardest of rocks posed a problem? It sounds like the King of Austria telling Mozart his music has too many notes. Drilling might prove more difficult, certainly not impossible.

There is the notion that the buildings would be too old to withstand the vibrations. First, the Metro goes down very deep. Ridiculously deep, despite the supposed need for a fallout shelter. Washington overkill. It would be nice, both for passengers and onlookers to see manifestations of it, like in New York, Boston, or Paris — a train is not shameful, quite attractive on the contrary, injecting life and rhythm into a city that could use more. Second, the buildings of far more ancient cities — London, Budapest, Madrid, Barcelona have well survived the vibrations, even though many of the latter might be better built.

Given the present situation, it would be costly to retrace the line, dig up Pennsylvania Avenue and M Street, but how about creating a station right by the Potomac River? A moving carpet could transport those wishing to enter the heart of Georgetown to a more convenient exit/entrance near Wisconsin and M. Something to think about, all you urban planners out there.

*    *    *

So I tell la belle Claire, whose lovely teeth are chewing on a cheese and broccoli sandwich opposite me.

"I suppose," she says.

Why can her conversation not be as scintillating as her eyes? Or the necklace she has strung around her neck tonight?

"It looks beautiful," I say, lifting it up between my thumb and forefinger.

"It's just broken glass," she answers, removing my hand.

"Anybody ever tell you look a little like Ingrid Bergman?"

"Pleeeease. I can't stand Ingrid Bergman."

"Oh? She's one of my favorite actresses."

"I'm not surprised."

"Why is that?"

"I don't know, you're just that type."

She giggles. She knows I am looking at her.

"Come on," she continues, "get those stars out of your eyes. I'm not worth it, I'm telling you. Oh, by the way, my father says to say hi."

"Tell him I'm looking for a job."

"That's between the two of you, okay?"

Like the other day, her wrists are bare, as are the knuckles of her tongue.

"Do you want to go for a stroll?" I suggest. The outside air will help.

"I suppose."

We walk out on the brick-laid sidewalk of Prospect Street. A car zooms by almost knocking me over.

"ASSHOLE!" I yell.

"Do you have to be so vulgar?" she asks.

"God, you don't say much, but when you do it's always to cut me down. This idiot almost killed me."

"But he didn't."

A taxi passes by — a Chrysler LeBaron, 1978. She hails it and gets into it, slams the door. I watch the scene as though someone were pouring a bottle of good Corbières wine down the sink. Good wine that never had time to breathe. I continue my stroll, still tasting the onions and oil on my breath.

I enter a bar blasting loud music into the street, order a draft at the bar and start talking with a woman sitting by herself looking into the distance, then at me, up and down. She has teased blonde hair and enough makeup on to stock a warehouse.

"Hello," I venture.

"How are you doing, or rather, *what* do you do?" she says.

"Funny you should ask. To answer the first part of the question: fine; now for the second part: I am unemployed and you, sweet thing?"

"Got to go to the bathroom."

"Have a good one."

"Go to hell, you piece of scum."

"Hey, nice to know you too."

*     *     *

Swallowed by the night, I return to 31st Street, introduce my key in the lock, open the door, flip on the light, look around. No letters, no messages. I think of Claire. How she eclipsed all the others; Deborah has faded like an old newspaper clipping; Charlotte Williamsburg never seems to have existed. I look back at the first days in Washington, remember Gloria. Sweet, intelligent Gloria. Do I still have her number? I leaf through a couple of address books. There it is. I dial.

"We're sorry, the number you have dialed has been disconnected."

Some nights were meant for sleep, and only sleep.

\*　　\*　　\*

The following day I park Balt on a lot off Nebraska, ride the L6 bus down Connecticut Avenue to the bustling downtown. I have a job interview. Or something rather that turns into an exercise in contempt as far as the interviewer is concerned.

"You're wasting my time, young man."

His arms are folded behind his head. As in a Miró painting little marks of perspiration dot his shirt behind which armpits lurk. He has pale grey eyes that have looked so much they cannot see anymore.

I walk away, looking down at the sidewalk, then raise my head as I pass a shop window on Connecticut when I see my reflection. Suddenly a feeling of nausea attacks me. Smack dab between the eyes, lodging itself more intensely in the left.

Look people: this man, although a college graduate, cannot get a good job, he is unemployed. Ah, ugly, awkward, dreaded word suddenly whistling in my ears with the intensity of a fire truck. Unemployed, not because of cutbacks. No, not I. Unemployed, because I got the boot. Laid off! Fired! I got the boot. Like some rogue, I was kicked in the buttocks.

The humiliation of it all! Perpetual, lingering. To see unemployment mirrored in the eyes of those who have a job and elevate themselves out of their own miasma by sneering at the likes of me. We are left to ourselves, forced into narcissism, sinking into the bowels of neurosis. Idleness does not help, but where to start?

I was told to go to hell. Funny how many expressions carry a literal, obvious, yet forgotten meaning. They descend from primeval times and are carried over from generation to generation, always there to be interpreted correctly. The word remains and thus the intrinsic meaning. It is the poet's role and duty to draw attention to the original sense. Too bad poetry does not bring home the bacon, or at least the imitation bacon bits.

I must capitalize on the eternal return. Yes, like the devil, I am free. And do I want to deal with all these jerks in Washington anyhow? These heinous apostles of the surface world? Give me a Grecian urn, that I may puke. Alas poor Mr. K.!

But, horns *et al*, I stand, in front of the shop window, gazing at a combination of my reflection and greeting cards. My God. Between the various shades of green of the Saint Patrick cards which have just replaced the pink and red love messages of Saint Valentine's Day, I see a blur with steel-rimmed eyeglasses, a mustache and long hair. Is that me? Hm. More of a mane than I had expected; *but,* I am dressed like *them*: red, slightly pointed alligator shoes; one of my father's most expensive 100 per cent silk neckties with blue and ocher lines striping an indigo background; my navy blue blazer; and my Burberry raincoat over it.

Perhaps *that is* what started it all. An insignificant detail. Never in my life have I worn one coat over another coat. Can you imagine? One coat over another coat? What a silly, useless thing to do! The first step toward oblivion and rejection of adolescent ideals. Such contempt I used to feel for adults who did that. They had sold out. It rubbed so much against the grain. So redundant, uncomfortable looking, absurd. Who is that doggie in the window? I am one of them. All decked out for an interview, most of which was spent at a receptionist's desk, the latter waving her hands about to dry her fingernails. I have to hold on to something. Adulthood is sucking me into its quagmire.

The image fades and whirls. I can see myself in ten years. One of *them*. Ah, the irony of the *me* generation, being actually anything but ME. Or me at my lowest. *Me* interviewing recent college graduates, asking them to sell themselves?

At least Mephistopheles conned Faust with style, and the old bugger did get a pretty good deal out of it. He could cavort with Marguerite, as opposed to getting stuck between asbestos rugs and an asbestos ceiling dotted with humming neon lights, faced with an in-tray and an out-tray, and people who not only are forced to be sandwiched in between the two, but like it. You can spot those who fake it. They don't get promoted and they don't stay in the capital city. They start tofu farms in Minnesota or something.

The reverie fades, the image swirls back to the present. Suddenly, I am back on Connecticut Avenue. Bored, discouraged, disgusted, terrified.

I step into *Ernie's* to rest my eyes on a couple of go-go dancers. Not bad for once. The woman on the right has a kind face. She looks at me as if knowingly; she's been there. She understands. Aside from a young black man sitting next to the stage, all I see are surface men, with sad gleaming eyes, ready to return to the office, wife, or Love Boat, after this mildly lascivious interlude.

"Be positive," old Darwell would say.

I pay for the Miller Lite draft and walk out. Burp. Phew; it sort of smelled in there. The outside air whips me pleasantly in the face. Such a pale sky. I pick up one of the city's free newspapers and take the L6 bus back up to Nebraska Avenue where Balthazar awaits.

Bumpety bump. I don't recall the European buses bouncing around like this. But I guess that certain forms of sloppiness comprise the charm of this nation. Perhaps it is simply the jerky bus that is exacerbating the nausea.

Perhaps: a gentle word, a word of doubt and mystery. A word that worries the surface man. I look around, they are all there: the contemptuous women, the loud teenagers, the lawyers. One of them, a little swarthy man, is actually picking his nose. There must be at least a couple of joints up there. Hey, buddy, need a hand? When the bus finally reaches Nebraska, I am dead.

\* \* \*

The Post informs one of its most faithful readers these days that a delicatessen in Bethesda is looking for a sandwich maker. I underline the phone number, call it up.

"You're the first one to call. Come on over," a woman with a Mexican accent tells me.

"Who should I ask for?"

"Ramona Menendez."

I will not blow this one. No, not I. I don my corduroy suit, choose my whitest shirt, my cleanest tie; type up a résumé highlighting my scholarly achievements, rather than my meager professional adventurism; and off I am. Before getting out of the car I comb my hair one last time in the rearview mirror. It is a little long and my beard is somewhat bushy. I look more like a figure out of Dostoyevsky than the 20th century. Oh, what is this woman going to think? And where is this deli anyway? Oh, I just walked past it. It is a minute recess in a big office building. Minute but clean.

"Mrs. Menendez?"

"Yeah?"

Ah, there she is, emerging from behind the counter.

A pink t-shirt and a black skirt emphasize her numerous pounds. A mop of straight black hair hides most of her forehead. She looks me up and down. Her eyebrows seem to rise a little. I hand her my résumé. See, I went to Burdon College; look, I was an editor for the literary magazine; notice, I speak fluent French and fairly acceptable Spanish. Perhaps I should have bought a sample paper or a photograph. A painting? How do you impress these people anyway?

"Have you ever prepared sandwiches before?" she asks.

The question takes me aback.

"Well, for myself. I've even invented one."

"Oh yeah?"

I can imagine the drum roll. This was not all in vain. Gold will be extracted from a barely significant detail. The newspapers are going to rush their top photographers over. NEW SANDWICH INVENTED! Read all about it!

She continues to peer at my résumé. Isn't she going to ask me at least what my sandwich is? But do I want to reveal my terrible secret so that she gets rich on my back? I have fallen for cheap tricks, but I have learned my lesson.

"Does this have your phone number?"

"Oh yes; see there on top?"

My right index shows the precise spot. Maybe I should tell her that I washed dishes.

"Yeah I see it. Okay, thanks for stopping by. I'll give you a call."

To my utmost surprise the call never came.

\* \* \*

I have had to leave the basement and set up quarters in the little room on the second floor because the house's fourth person has moved in. Lily. She is an older woman with a big, slightly asymmetric bottom, a strong, rather pointed chin, high forehead, and a somewhat manic smile. She drove all the way from Utah in a pea-green Toyota station wagon with her even older parents. She has spent time in Europe, and

Spain in particular, but is somehow more for the American way than Superman himself. The American way and community.

"But don't you feel the American way has eroded community?"

"No, that's the foreign influence."

"But you've lived overseas. Surely, there's more of a spirit of community in Spain than here."

"There is still a strong Arab influence in Spain, especially in the south. Andalucia."

"That's as may be, but the family is alive, which is more than you can say here. Everyone eating separately, the system encourages people to dine alone, drive alone, do everything alone. It's very lucrative for industry but the consequence is the death of the community and the rise of crime."

"You didn't grow up here, did you?" she says with a grin. She knows.

"No, but I can see what is happening now. If any country has any influence on others it's America. Through movies, television, fast food, soft drinks, clothes... Besides you've spent a lot of time abroad too."

"Twenty years."

A semi-rueful smile flutters to her lips, or is it nostalgia for those two decades?

"See?" I put rhetorically.

"But I was with my parents and they're both American."

The old ploy of trying to out-American thy neighbor.

"Don't you lose some of your Americanness as you live overseas?" I wonder.

"No. You're quite American too in some ways."

Her accent is broad like the Midwestern plains. Maple syrup to the ear.

"But not overly enthralled with the American way."

"It's a shame."

A hint of sparkle has vanished from her eyes.

"I think it's a shame you are not more attuned to what is happening around you."

"Oh, but I am."

Again that grin, both sad and witch-like. We are talking in the small dining room, a dull light reverberates from the ceiling. Outside one can distinguish the areola of a street lamp.

"What brought you to Washington?" I ask, switching subjects. Part of me wants to punch her big bottom. One-two, whack-whack.

"The job market. I type very fast, have a Masters in Spanish. I also speak some French. It's an international city. It's exciting!"

"How is the job search?"

"Very good. I'm working for a Temp agency."

"What's that?"

"A place that hires temporary and mainly office help. It's something you might be interested in doing. You speak several languages and you type, don't you?"

*Crime and Punishment* is nearing the end, it is time to inject new blood into my professional life, so I have filled out an application and taken a test for the Tempox Temporary Agency. Eat your heart out, these people recognize my talent: I know every single letter of the alphabet, as a matter of fact I can count and spell "much better than average, especially considering the fact that you are an English major and that somehow they usually spell the worst." But my typing is not incredibly fast by Washington standards, where the fastest typists of the civilized world congregate.

*

# XIX

# A GLIMMER

The red telephone of my small bedroom rings. 8:15. My God, who could be calling at this ungodly hour?

"Hello?"

"HI! Is this Albert?"

"Yeah."

"HI! This is Zoysia from Tempox Temps! I've got an assignment for you!"

"You do?"

"YES! Let me tell you a little bit about it."

I wait with bated breath, thinking about the joy it will be to brush my teeth.

With a navy blue and tan necktie tightened around my shirt collar, my hair drying from my most recent shower, my fresh breath, I take the bus downtown, walk over to the place I have jotted down on a magazine renewal slip: Cohen, Goldberg and Shapiro Law Firm on L Street. I look around as the crowd bustles, rediscovering active life, Washington-city-of-work. Who cares if the women are wearing sneakers to cover their stockinged feet? I am back in the swing of things and in the elevator leading to the 11th floor. There it is at the end of the hallway, next to a most unfortunately locked Men's Room. I push a thick glass door open, the type my father would perennially bang into because he had failed to notice the treacherous surface. A very pretty black woman, whose lower body is hidden by a narrow, curving contraption which looks more like a podium than a desk, tells me to have a seat.

"I just returned from Louisville," she says with a big warm smile. "See, that's where I'm from originally. They just restored this old theater. I went down there to see a show with my cousins. It was beautiful. Funny, just like in the past, the whites sat down below and the blacks up top. Of course it doesn't have to be that way anymore but old habits are hard to break."

The morning sun caresses her turquoise blouse.

"You know," she goes on, "I'm trying so hard to lose weight. I think I've already taken off 20 pounds."

I see her slender face; nothing about her chest suggests excess.

"But you're not fat at all. Really."

Some people are paranoid.

"Oh yes I am. Wait 'till I stand up."

She pulls away from her desk and turns around. Her behind! My goodness, it looks as though she has stuffed a couple of pillows down her pants.

"See what I mean?"

"You're still a very pretty woman. You look a little like Mannix's secretary."

"Thank you."

A young white woman appears. Short blonde hair, ruffled collar, sneakers.

"Are you the temp?" she asks.

"I am Albert Nostran."

"Okay, yeah, come with me."

She gives instructions on legal documents to file.

"Do you follow me?"

Actually, the instructions are explained in a rather nebulous way, and perhaps my face strikes a puzzled expression, but common sense fills in the gaps. Down I go on my knees, praying this job will not last forever. At least I am working, I tell myself. Pretty soon I am shuffling papers away, like a gambler on the Mississippi. My knowledge of the alphabet really comes in handy and I get a whole half hour for lunch after which I am kindly greeted by the receptionist's better half. I come home by the 5:45 bus feeling as though rats have dug holes through one of my cerebral hemispheres to get to the other.

On the fourth day of this activity, which I may chalk up to experience, I am about to leave the wall-to-wall carpeted premises when a fellow in overalls strikes up a conversation. In the elevator. I respond. He seems surprised and a smile appears below his mustache. Elevators were meant to go up and down, not for talking.

"Hey, can I buy you a beer?" He says.

"Sure."

I follow him to what I assume will be a bar. No, it's a liquor store. He buys two Buds, has them wrapped in a brown bag. We walk over to McPherson Square.

"This bench suit you?" he asks.

"Okay."

Cheers.

\*     \*     \*

A week later, I am stuffing envelopes for a non-profit organization up on 18<sup>th</sup> Street. One of the fellows with me says: "Wouldn't it be nice if this job could last at least until the end of the year?"

I look up at him, out the window at the street. It is a dreary, humid day. They are restoring a building on the other side. Good. How much more civilized than tearing things down all the time. Return to work. Until the end of the year. Jesus.

\*     \*     \*

Then, on the following day, I am sent to Rosslyn across the river to photocopy a couple of million pages. I should have worn sunglasses and lead in my jacket because I feel that the machine's green light is either going to make me blind or riddle my body with plutonium. This is even worse than stuffing envelopes. I attempt to use the two-side feature but a couple of documents get muddled up. So my boss tells me. Her boss comes over to me. Somehow he knows that I speak French. His is not bad, unlike the handshake he gives me as he departs, during which one of his fingers proceeds to tickle my palm. And we have hardly been introduced.

\*     \*     \*

The next assignment, if I accept it, is to number pages on legal documents in a very important case involving a major telephone company. This tape will self-destruct within the next five seconds. I hang up the receiver, don my Ray-Bans and off I am. To Capitol Hill. To a building with no windows. A handsome structure that would make Hitler's bunker look like a rococo extravaganza. Our supervisor is a man with curly brown hair, eyeglasses, and a mustache, who has not seen the light of day since he was 14. His skin is translucent like an embryo's.

He compliments one of my co-workers who indeed seems to be performing the job with unusual zeal. She cocks her chest with pleasure. For half a second I consider a bestial gesture. No; too many pages to count. Another page-numberer is fired: an older man who just lost a 20-year old government position and started to get confused with the numbers. Those little boogers are indeed easy to miss. The chest-cocker has been appointed sub-supervisor and points out to me that I left out page 1,237. That will not happen again, please have mercy.

"My dream is to open a 7-11 store," says a third co-worker.

Mine is to find another line of work before I lose my marbles.

*   *   *

The following week, I decide to turn down a job, and take the day off. I have decided to start *The Brothers Karamazoff.* And suddenly Tempox has nothing to offer me anymore. Every day, I call.

"Sorry, nothing's going on."

"Well, how the hell do you stay in business?"

"Call us in a week. And do watch your language."

"Up yours."

I contact other agencies. Temple Temps sends me over to a newly erected building on Pennsylvania Avenue with huge windows. My goal is to clean up a basement full of sheet-plaster. At least I am away from stuffy offices and wall-to-wall carpeting, not crouched on a desk under some humming fluorescent light; I am using my body. Ah.

One of the men working with me just lost his position as an accountant; he is wearing a white shirt and his pants look as though they were the lower half of a suit. Hardly less appropriate, mind you, than applying as a sandwichist in an even more elaborate attire. His hands shake as he wrestles with the weight of the sheet-plaster boards. At the end of the day he begins dropping his load at more regular intervals. That night as I return home, I crack open a beer and turn on an imaginary TV. Oh, good, right in time for the commercial.

*   *   *

Heeding my mother's advice I have taken the Orange Line out to Ballston to meet Fred Gulan, the successful journalist son of old Mrs. Gulan, the widow of one of father's old friends, thanks to whom my parents settled in Stone Harbor.

"It can't do you any harm. You cannot do these clerical tasks all your life. You've got to pull your socks up."

"You're right. How's Pop?"

"Better than ever."

"Maybe I can come up in a bit."

"That would be wonderful; I'm sure he would be happy to see you too."

"Give him my love."

Droves of commuters pour out of the subway, now to walk home or catch a bus for a yet more distant destination. Other people are being welcomed by their loved ones. Though I do not know him, certainly not well enough to love him, Gulan is going to come and get me.

I once saw him on a program on Latin America and remember a tall forehead coinciding with a receding hairline. I thought this was one of the worst television performances I had ever seen. It was not so much what he said but how he said it that bothered me: a weak, whiny, plebeian voice which explained why he had gotten into writing the news from behind the camera.

There he is, walking toward me. Quite tall and more impressive in person. They say the camera makes you gain weight but he seems a lot heavier than when I saw him a month ago. It is of course conceivable that he has eaten a lot since then or has been struck with a thyroid problem.

He shakes my hand vigorously. We walk towards his car.

"So you used to work with Mouluvert? Dominique and I go way back; covered the Watergate together."

He sounds enthusiastic; someone who really loves his job.

A wife, Natalia, and a child, Titipoo, await as he pulls the Pontiac into the driveway. She is of Croatian origin and refuses to consider herself a Yugoslav.

"I speak a language similar to Serbian but I have little in common with those people."

The little boy smiles, hides his face in his hands, and then runs up the stairs.

"What are you having Albert? Scotch? Gin and tonic?"

"Scotch will be fine."

The ice cubes rattle pleasantly around the glass.

"I hear your father is not doing so well..."

"Actually, every time I talk to my mother, there seems to be some improvement."

"That's good to hear. Your father and mine were in the same business; there isn't anything like it. You know how I started out?"

"No."

But I soon will.

"Freelancing."

"Oh."

"Yeah, stringing for the Christian Scientosophist in Peru. Washington is chock full of correspondents, but a lot of papers in the world can't afford to send their own man so they rely on press agencies."

"Like the Universal Wire Service."

"For instance. But believe me, a lot of organizations would be delighted to receive more news..."

"Dinner is ready," the wife announces. In the background, the television can be heard.

"My God! What was that?"

Gulan rushes from the table.

"But Fred, it's going to get cold."

"I don't give a shit! Let me hear what's on TV."

I follow him.

"I can't believe it; there's a coup in Spain! Some military have attempted to take over the Parliament. This is big stuff!"

He flips the channel from CBS to NBC to ABC. The picture shows a large amphitheater; in the middle stands a man with a huge mustache, sporting the Guardia Civil's three-cornered hat, *el sombrero de tres picos* or *tricornio,* not Emiliano Zapata or Pancho Vila but Antonio Tejero, driving a wedge between Adolfo Suarez, the first democratically elected president since the Civil War, and his successor Leopoldo Calvo Sotelo. Tejero brandishes a gun, while the communists crouch under their benches. He shoots up in the air.

*"¡QUE SE SIENTEN, COÑO[17]!"*

"This is it," says Gulan.

It seems too sudden, too impromptu.

I feel I am back at the Universal Wire Service, back between the news's cancerous, nicotine-smeared lungs. Excitement and filth go hand in smudgy hand.

---

17   -Sit down, goddamn it!

"It might start all over again, like in '36. It was too good to last, just as the world thought Spain was a European country like any other."

Like France = Germany = Italy = Britain = Denmark. Journalists are sometimes silly. The seed of freelancing remains in my mind as I wave goodbye to Natalia. Titipoo is already sound asleep in a world yet unperturbed by headlines, by-lines, guidelines, and sidelines. Gulan drives me back to the Metro. His high forehead glistens as the moon and stars dot a sky not overly invaded by mercury-vapor lights.

*       *       *

That night in my narrow bed, in my narrow room, I have a curious dream.

*"You have been appointed Governor of California,"* Mouluvert *tells me.*

*I stare at his bald head pleasantly highlighted by the morning rays. I am not sure whether to take this as a compliment or not, though to be governor of California is certainly not the worst thing that could happen to me.*

*We shake hands.*

*"Thank you very much," I say.*

*Nice glow, Moulu-Moulu.*

*Pfff. I am zonked, ready to die or at least to forget. I climb on the elevator. A ticket awaits on the windshield. Another one for my collection. I raise my eyebrows, start the engine, and drive off in Balthazar back to Park Mapletree.*

*After I open the door to my duplex, I find roomie Gronket, at the dining-room table, stuffing himself with Chicken Kiev, one of many exotic meals he loves to prepare for himself, his eyes darting all over the place, hoping, praying that no one will come around to share it. An elaborate form of masturbation I think to myself, while yelling out a perfectly insincere "hello."*

*"Hllm," Gronket answers back, to my delight half-choking. Cough-cough.*

*I try to tell him about my night at work, and of course about the puzzling news, but he is obviously eager to be left alone with his meal. No time to even discuss the Smothers Brothers Show and Top Forty Music. Ha!*

*Feeling increasingly drowsy, I leave Fred and his edible partner, and walk up the two flights of steps to my room. I lie down on my big double bed, but sleep will not come, greatly because Davey Gronket downstairs has, considerate fellow that he is, started listening to the radio. This is hardly the first time. Despite certain noticeable patterns Davey still does not understand that I work at night. All he understands is himself, which demands no brainstorm. My new appointment — G. of C. — cannot convince me that moderation is the key to all woes. Not this one.*

*It has become imperative that I beat him up. Boy do I ever hate getting out of bed. And so unnecessarily! Having no slippers, I put my wing-tips back on and strut down the stairs. Kaplonk-kaplonk-kaplonk. I do not care if the combination of shoes and (navy blue) pajamas looks unusual.*

*"Okay mother, put up your dukes," I say.*

*He looks disdainfully from his plate.*

*"Tsk. That's such an outdated expression. You really talk funny!"*

*"Screw you."*

*In two seconds flat I have him out of his chair and pinned to the floor. But it feels as though I am tackling a spider. Davey's limbs seemed to have doubled in number.*

*"Feisty little bugger, aren't you? Now stop that!"*

*"Let me go! You hear? Let me go!" the diner whined.*

*"Shut up!"*

*I whack him a good one. POW!*

*Ah, the joy to see him merciless on the living room floor. The cringing little bastard.*

*I must have hit him just a little too hard for as I look down at him, I suddenly notice his neck — the tennis pro's neck he was so proud of — is now crooked. Uh-oh. Is this physically possible? Even though I have no precise means of measurement, the angle must be a good 30 degrees, instead of, well, being straight like the average human neck tends to be. I cannot help but smile. I ask the motionless body:*

*"Wake up, little Davey. Yoo-hoo!" Oh, what's the use. Little Davey was never to wake up, and thus pester anybody ever again.*

*The following days a certain number of people came to resent the fact: "How could you do that?" "Such a grand cook!" etc.*

*"I'm sort of puzzled myself, to tell you the truth; but let's look at the brighter side: I'll finally be able to sleep without being disturbed. Honestly, was Davey Gronket's life that important?"*

*A deployment of candidness which is met with an onslaught of hypocrisy.*

*About a week and three days later, I run into Rachel in downtown, where the old Y.M.C.A. used to stand and where Haitians now sell chocolate chip cookies. She begins to swear at me. On the verge of hysterics she tells me that I had no right to kill Davey, even if he did make too much noise and liked to eat by himself, etc.*

*I smile benevolently: had I not been named Governor of California?*

\* \* \*

King Juan Carlos I de Borbón y Borbón, Franco's unpredictable heir with the high forehead and the Greek wife, has intervened. After keeping members of Parliament up all night, the rebels have surrendered. The tanks which had started to roam the streets of Valencia can return to the barracks. Mr. coup leader, Antonio Tejero with the big mustache, on the other hand, will not pass GO, collect 20,000 pesetas, and head directly to jail. Or almost, since a trial will take place.

The inauguration ceremony continued and old Calvo Sotelo was sworn in after all. Democracy is in Spain to stay.

\* \* \*

My romantic life however is wallowing in utter darkness. Claire can go crawl down some sewer pipe. How can someone so physically attractive be so emotionally cold and so intellectually unstimulating? Mystery and gumball. Why does she not channel her imagination into something else than teasing? I am no longer in high school! I tried, it did not work, so be it. Adieu.

My guide to night places recommends a couple of clubs on 19th Street down from Dupont Circle. One of them is *Peter's Pack*. I see the sign written in bright orange letters against a rustic piece of wood. On the neighboring sidewalk stands a hot dog vendor. So this is where young adults go. And only young adults, or somewhat older ones attempting to pass. Cars roll down the hill bumper to bumper, the first quest of the night is the parking space. Streams of people stroll by. Girls walk together, a few men walk in couples too. For some reason I am surprised to never run into any person from the Universal Wire Service. Where do these people hang out?

I walk inside, look around. The place smells of wood and sawdust. Bamboo paneling graces the walls virtually up to the Styrofoam ceiling which is dotted with spotlights. People are playing backgammon on high stools, the music is 1980s top-forty; from time to time an older song bursts forth; it is to the ear what cold water is to the parched throat; there is a small circular dance floor and a disc-jockey in a booth. I stroll around the room; there are hundreds of Polaroid shots dating back to some recent bash. I am reminded of Baudelaire lambasting photography. *The people, like one Narcissus...* Most are acting or posing as though for a cigarette commercial. Suave, sophisticated, wordily. *Mondain*, the French say, which sounds like the English "mundane," perhaps appropriately. Although I spent a summer in Wyoming among cowboys, sage brush, and dust, I am reluctant to act like the Marlboro man. I feel like seltzer water dropping inside a vat of Bourbon.

Instead, I order a Tom Collins at a tiny opening at the bar. The bartender has a copy of the collected works of Kant in his back pocket. Men and women are flirting, exchanging the right lines, speaking the words that push the right buttons. It is like a play performed at a community center. Like an article in *Cosmopolitan Magazine* come to life. In this mess I spot an attractive blonde in a white outfit sitting alone on her stool.

"Do you want to dance?" I ask her.

Conversation strikes me as superfluous.

"Not really."

"Why not?"

"I've got a wooden leg."

A likely tale.

"I'm sorry."

"That's alright."

"How did it happen?"

"A shark bit it off one day I went scuba diving."

Such a vivid imagination! Do you still explore the deep or does the wood prevent you from reaching the bottom?

"How gruesome. You seem well-balanced though."

"I try."

Should I ask if I may touch? If only for good luck? Knock-knock. I try to picture her in an 18th century English port, with a parrot perched on her right shoulder, yelling "pieces of eight," but the conversation seems to be faltering. I do not detect much interest on her part and mine is failing too. As in Baudelaire's *The Madman and the Venus*, the statue with her marble eyes is looking at something afar. But there are other statues in this garden. A former salesman, I do not abandon the game that easily; I shall not take "no" for an answer! A fast Elvis number comes on.

*Scratch my back, run your pretty fingers through my hair...*

My kind of music. Inspiration tickles my brain. My adrenalin is pushing against the Tennessee Valley Authority dam of pent-up frustration. My hair rises to a pompadour. It is all I can do to prevent my legs and pelvis from swaying involuntarily from one corner of the room to the other. I ask a second woman if she wishes to sway to the king's rhythm.

She is a little more plump than Long John Silver and her inner beauty is such that it overflows on the outside. She is medium height with droopy blue eyes where one detects a hint of past pain, full lips, and a pleasant shape. I like the way her red suspenders shape her bosom and how her red curly hair frames her round face. Positively more attractive than average. She says no but her eyes: "Please stay. Don't listen to those meaningless words."

"What do you do?" she asks. The Washington question, I have been told.

"I write."

"Oh you do? That's interesting. Who do you write for?"

"No one in particular. I'm a freelancer. Are you sure you don't want to dance?" I have to shout in her ear because the music is loud, particularly because of the bass. A man jostles me, says he is sorry.

"No, not right now. By the way, my name is Sandra."

"Albert."

We shake hands.

"What do you do Sandra?"

"I'm an executive secretary, but right now I'm also organizing a show for a sculptor."

Have you posed for him? I wonder.

"That sounds interesting."

"I'm trying to get the press interested but so far there hasn't been much response."

"Like who?"

"The Post, the Star, the Washingtonian, a bunch of others."

"Hmm. Maybe I could write something."

"Really?" she looks at me with those intriguing blue eyes. "That would be so fantastic."

Sandra is with a taller girlfriend with long blonde hair — which I suspect is dyed. She eyes me suspiciously and makes sarcastic comments now and then. Suddenly the lights dim, the music slows.

"I think I would like to dance now," Sandra says.

My heart leaps forth, my teeth feel as though they are about to fall out.

She presses her body against mine. Most of me is saying yes-yes but paradoxically the most enthusiastic organ is pushing this most pleasant lass away. The drink is rising to my head and her mouth is rising to my lips. My fingers comb her curls. The ceiling is spinning around like a merry-go-round. Happy days are here again.

A half-hour later, as the bar is closing, I find my way to the door. A skinny guy with a yellow complexion and a beard who looks as though he has just arrived from a village in West Virginia tells me: "I've got a date for next Friday."

"I've got an interview."

\* \* \*

"AMERICA IS THE GREATEST COUNTRY IN THE WORLD!" a man with a black beard yells on the other side of the street. He is walking in a most creative way. Like a knight on a chessboard.

The building behind is Flip's, where Claire and I savored our first beer. Together. To quote the word she liked to hear.

*   *   *

I have managed to park big Balthazar on U Street Northwest in front of one of the townhouses which has recently been restored. I walk up a couple of flights of stairs. Sandra greets me in a short black velvety dress and white stockings, looking most appetizing. We walk around the room full of silvery stainless-steel soldered squares, spirals, corkscrews, circles, and floral-inspired shapes. Some even come equipped with a small motor.

She introduces me to Roberto Morassi, the sculptor from Uruguay. He is a little man with a salt and pepper goatee, bald in a sort of becoming way. His eyes are quick, black, and bright, but I am struck by his serenity.

We walk over to a couch and I take out a pen and pad. As he talks I scribble down notes.

"I started as a painter, but one day as I was walking down this back alley, I came across this mechanic who was using a blow torch. It was fascinating. I asked him if I could use it, he accepted, and I have not really put it down since."

Perspiration is pouring down from my armpits while I am attempting to keep a composed exterior. From time to time Sandra struts by, checking to see if all is well.

"I'm sure your work has been compared to Calder's."

Morassi tilts his head to the side, smiles.

"I'm not sure whether Calder was really conscious of what he was doing, and though I admire his work greatly, I think I might have taken it a step further."

After Morassi has shaken my hand and taken off, Sandra comes up to me with a big smile and her big blue eyes.

"I came with a friend and I don't have a car; I was wondering if you could drive me home tonight?"

Balthazar, Sandra and I plunge over the Potomac into Virginia, down 395, past the Pentagon, past Shirlington, past Park Mapletree. How is life, Gronket? Enjoying the Grand Duke of Luxembourg? Recent memories ooze to the surface. I see signs that say Richmond; the lights on the road swirl like radioactive onions. They dance to the song of the night. I think of Claire. With whom I wanted to tour the world and live the rest of my life. Lovely Claire, but adolescent, cruel Claire who took my heart for an apple and bit a big chunk out of it.

We swerve onto the Duke Street exit, after a couple of commercial blocks, we turn into suburbia and weave through the labyrinth up to a one-story brick house outside which a couple of trees stand guard. The air of the night is fragrant. I feel extra-terrestrials are about to land.

"Well... Here we are," she says. "Would you like to come in?"

"Sure."

She bends to unlock the front door.

"This is it. Come on in."

Posters of sunsets and mountain lakes greet us. Elegant words of wisdom are inscribed on them to enable one to lead a fuller, richer, thicker life.

"Have a seat. Would you like some wine?" Sandra asks.

"Do you have any red?"

"No, only white, I'm afraid."

White sometimes prevents me from sleeping and can give me a headache when it's too fruity.

"White is fine. By the way, what town is this?"

"Technically, it's Annandale."

Technically. We are back in the burbs.

We are sitting on the couch when her roommate, the tall sarcastic blonde, comes in with a man slightly shorter than her with a beard and a grin revealing imperfect teeth. They soon disappear into the basement and when the wine is but a memory at the bottom of our two glasses I lift Sandra up and carry her to her bedroom. Once on her feet again she unzips her velvety black dress while I sit on the bed and start to untie my shoelaces. I also have a beard and a grin. And something not unlike the leaning tower of Pisa.

*

## XX

# HORIZONS NOUVEAUX

L ast evening proved so fulfilling that I return to Sandra's the following night. There is, however, a variation to the theme: Sandra's two boys are back from their father's house. Roy and Roger.

"Hi, Fellers."

"G"

"L"

While the mother has in recent years become a vegetarian, there is little her two sons enjoy more than steak. Roy, the older one, is eleven and has a tan complexion and black hair; Roger, the younger, seven, could be my son: rosy cheeked and blonde. Both are obnoxious little brats. Small wonder: Sandra gives in to their every whim.

"Mom, go get me some ketchup!" whines Roy.

"Shouldn't you say please?"

"Okay. PLEASE!"

"Can I have some ketchup too?" Roger challenges.

"That's *may* I have some ketchup too," I say.

This has neither endeared me to the children nor to their mother. Sometimes it takes so very little for the yarn to unravel. She now ignores me and I have difficulty wracking my brains to come up with brilliant conversation.

"I think it would be better that we not see each other for a while. With the kids, it's so difficult."

"I understand. Goodbye."

"Keep me posted about the article."

"No problem."

And off into the night, with Balthazar. Easy come, easy go.

\*   \*   \*

Michael Kent

On my way back I decided to stop on K Street. I stepped into a large store which was full of prostitutes walking around big white refrigerators. I did my best to ignore the women of the night and they ignored me too. One of them reminded me of Sandra's roommate.

Shortly after, I drove off and headed for the nearest highway.

As the early dawn rose I was still driving. The freeway had become huge. Judging by the wide open spaces around me and the sagebrush covered hills, I was out west somewhere. Maybe Wyoming. I liked the idea of being out west early in the morning, all alone.

Further along the road I noticed what I thought to be a toll. I stopped at a sort of rest area just before it.

A man with a mustache and a brown uniform came up to the car. He told me he wanted to see my papers before I went to Canada. I walked over to a change machine. The dirty gold coins were francs if I was to believe the large "Fs" on them.

The officer smiled at me and said it was alright for me to leave.

\*    \*    \*

Another sun-filled day. I have returned to Carl's desk, my notes are to my left, and a sheet of onion-skin paper is in the typewriter. I have also torn out a review from the *Washington Post's* Style section to see how their critic operates. I type a couple of lines, look at the result, tear the sheet out, crumple it up, and throw it into the wastepaper basket. I have seen it done in movies. Traditionally I have always handwritten a first draft, but it is time I adapt to the Hemingway school of prose.

Four attempts lay like origami aborted fetuses in the trashcan but the fifth is coming along. My brain and my fingers are enjoying the exercise. One page, two pages, three pages, four. The End. I reread it, nod to myself. Show it to Carl and Flora. They like it too, even though they did not like a short story I had shown them a couple of weeks earlier. On the other hand, if they liked everything I could not rely on their judgment.

I read the whole thing on the telephone to Sandra.

*If Roberto Morassi and his stainless steel sculptures could be fitted into some kind of convenient niche, it would probably have the shape of a pentagon. And why a pentagon? The best qualified entity to ask would be Mother Nature, for it is she who sprinkles the magic five-sided shape from petals to leaves to beehive cells. It is she who can be venerated for what Morassi calls the vital, or divine proportion.*

*Though Morassi's name might not ring an immediate bell, the Uruguayan artist, who prefers the coziness of Alexandria to the troublesome political skies of his own country, has been exhibiting off and on since 1946. His artistic endeavors have led him from Montevideo to Washington, via Paris, Munich, Rome and Barcelona, always in quest of the divine proportion or what makes the perfect work of art.*

*It was, however, in a back-alley garage in the mid-fifties, that the mild mannered Uruguayan was struck by light: "I was fascinated by the mechanic's torch, I asked him if I could use it, which he accepted after a while. It seems I have never really put it down since. Before that I was a painter."*

*And from that day on, Morassi has steadily and prolifically developed his art. His sculptures have become popular, namely with architects, who welcome their simplicity, warmth, and power as a necessary humanizing touch to contrast with their steel and glass structures.*

*The warmth and energy immediately comes to mind when observing the shiny paraphernalia of rings, spirals, corkscrews and various metallic plants which enliven Morassi's ascetic studio.*

*In almost every piece on display, one can perceive what one critic called "rhythmic and endless motion." One of his most intriguing (and expensive) works, "The Dance of Seven Rings," is actually propelled by a small motor which whimsically turns on and off.*

*It is quite tempting to compare Morassi's ribbons of steel with Alexander Calder's "Mobiles." When he hears this, the sculptor-mechanic tilts his head to one side, smiles and says, "I am not really sure whether Calder was really conscious of what he was doing, and although I admire his work greatly,, I think I might have taken it a step farther by creating a sense of volume in space."*

*Morassi remains abstract, or rather a "non-representationalist" to use his words, and shies away from literal interpretations of his art. "People always see things in my work I never dreamt of putting there," he said.*

Michael Kent

*In an age that has proclaimed the death of art, or at least of so-called "bourgeois art" fir to please the eye, the Uruguayan turned Alexandrian thinks in terms of aesthetics. "I think art should be beautiful," he said. I believe in man. Let's say that my sculptures are characteristic of humanity and of life."*

"I love it."

Her voice almost sounds like that of a child's. With tears in my eyes I remember how she nibbled on me. But that is something that will not reoccur.

Now the part I dislike: mailing it. I try *The Post*, the *Washingtonian*, the *Washington Weekly*. That should do it.

\* \* \*

A week elapses. Temple Temps has sent me to M.C.I., a new telephone company that needs to get its mailroom sorted out. I join a woman and two black fellows swimming through several tons of mail.

My contact is Jay Kruger, a friendly chap who comes around once in a while to see how we are.

"I know it's rough to work in a room with no windows and I sincerely apologize."

The woman, Sarah, seems to be in her early thirties; she is slender, her face is twisted in a funny way, but she seems to like me. The first black man, Gregory, leaves us after the first day; the other, George, is very light skinned and has green eyes.

"You must have a lot of white blood," Sarah tells him.

"No, I don't."

"How come you have green eyes and pale skin?"

"It's because I have a Comanche ancestor."

Sarah looks at me. The Comanches and their famous green eyes. But he is a nice man, taking night classes to become an accountant.

"You have a strange accent," he tells Sarah.

"It's not an accent, it's a speech impediment. I was born with a harelip."

"Nothing wrong with that. Actually, it sounds sort of distinguished."

"I took speech therapy to improve."

\* \* \*

Last night, I talked with Salvador Dalí. He was very friendly and said he liked my paintings, which were very true to his own surrealistic code.

*   *   *

One by one the publications to which I have mailed my piece on Morassi have returned it. I call Sandra.

"Well, since the artist lives in Alexandria, you could always try the *Alexandria Gazette*."

The *Gazette*. Sounds like a cheap publication, or at least old-fashioned; certainly does not have the ring or the prestige of *The Washington Post*.

First I call them up. The woman who answers me has the charm of a wounded gorilla.

"It's something we might use," she growls. "Send it over."

*   *   *

Flora, who is a bit of a Francophile, has a box in the attic full of French books. They have a pleasant musty smell to them. Finding a good book in an attic is one of the joys of life. I read Gide's *The Immoralist*, *The Vatican's Cellars*, Camus's *The Plague*, after which I pick up *Manon Lescaut* by L'Abbé Prévost. It tells in that wonderful, light, playful 18th century style how the Chevalier des Grières is led around by the collar and teased by the heroine. One day she seems to love him desperately, the next she is running off to conquer some new horizons.

Speaking of which, I have not left the city in quite some time. It is quite obvious that Sandra does not want me and while it hurts a little, it is not the quasi metaphysical pain I felt after being tossed around like a basketball between Claire Mouluvert's fins. For half a second I am tempted to call her: "Hi, Claire want to go to South Carolina and get a tan?" Resist, Albert, resist!

I search through my address book. Dare I? I did lie to her and she does live far away. I look out the window. A car drives by. Not that big a lie and not that far away and far enough to be interesting. With sweaty fingers I dial the number. A feminine voice with a winsome southern accent answers the phone.

"Jillian?"

"No, please wait a second. I'll go and get her."

Obviously a woman not raised by Sandra. Courtesy is like good Mozart.

"Hello?"

"Jillian?"

"My God, is this Albert?"

Apparently I must have a very recognizable voice.

"Yes, it's me. I have returned to Washington..."

Her voice has enough lilt to trigger manly sensations. It is nice to hear it, bringing back memories of the Hirshhorn museum, of my fledgling career as a graveyard shift journalist. I can almost picture her red hair.

"Oh? How was Boston?"

Ha.

"Not bad, but it had its limitations. Living at home and everything. My skills are better adapted to Washington's."

"I would imagine, but oooooh, it's so good to hear from you! Maybe you'd like to come down to Richmond this weekend?"

"J... It sounds splendid."

Is life beautiful or what?

"Let me give you directions."

Before she has time to say anything more I hang up the phone with a big smile in the middle of my beard. Actually I do have very precise directions. I pick up Don Pedro de la Guitarra, release the pick from under the strings, and strum a few songs, including "Mother," by John Lennon. Springtime is here.

Impetuosity gets the better of me. I take off my corduroys and shirt and don my shorts and sneakers, attempt to touch my toes, which makes my rear end feel most peculiar. Albert Nostran is going to go jogging for the first time since college. One-two, one-two. A Bach fugue, *takatakatakatakatakataka*, leaps into my skull and does not want to move out of it. But I cannot afford to dawdle, for tonight, for the first time since I have moved into my modest quarters, Carl and Flora have invited me to join them for dinner. I can't miss that. I return after a couple of miles, feeling drained but happy.

I shower, wash my hair with this new shampoo called "conditioner," which does not seem to wash much but leaves my hair very manageable. Should I wear a necktie? Should I wear anything at all? Carl and Flora are very liberal — it is actually surprising they have not invited me as the member of a threesome. The temperature is such that I would not catch a cold. When in doubt, refrain, so I sing another song on the guitar. My calluses are getting very thick.

Nothing like soggy vegetables and boiled chicken, downed with ice tea. I stare at the lemon, imprisoned between two ice cubes, melting slowly, thinking of my mother's Sunday roast. In France.

The 40-watt light bulb glistens timidly over the round table in the dining room, adding charm and atmosphere. How about a game of Russian roulette? Flora is dressed in green. Cotton turtleneck sweater and pants slightly flared at the bottom. I do not think I have ever seen her wear anything else. I wonder what she looks like naked. Carl is sporting a chamois green shirt and white painter pants. He also must have a wardrobe full of similar items.

"I bet that's a change from the corn-out-of-a-can and mayo sandwiches on white bread," the merry hostess quips.

"I never touch white bread anymore, now that I know the virtues of whole-wheat."

"Sorry."

Chuckle-chuckle.

She displays her perfect incisors. It seems as though her mouth only contains incisors. Like certain bovines. Carl, on the other hand, has very small, rodent-like teeth. He must grind them away during his sleep.

I stare sadly at the iced-tea. Do you have anything to perk it up? I knew I should have bought that bottle of rosé when I saw it in the store only a few hours ago. We could have at least drunk to our friendship.

"It's funny how in America you serve the salad before the main course," I say.

"Oh, that's right," says Flora, "in France, it's after the entrée."

"Speaking of which, the *entrée* is the first course."

"Isn't that interesting," comments Carl placing a hairy fist over his mouth to suppress a burp.

I am less skillful than he at suppressing secret pining.

"Too bad there's no wine."

"Yeah, Flora, what's happening?" Carl pursues.

"Next time, guys."

"I'll have some as soon as you serve the salad," says Carl.

"Actually," I say, "in theory, you're not supposed to drink wine with salad."

"Why's that?"

"I guess it's something to do with the fact that the dressing is prepared with vinegar, sour wine so to speak, and that would hinder your full appreciation of the wine."

"Is it real bad etiquette?"

I shrug my shoulders.

"Probably would demonstrate a lack of breeding."

"Then I'll make sure when I go to France to always drink wine with the salad."

Carl, you irreverent demon. I slap him on the back, and as a result he coughs out a vegetable which goes shooting toward Flora who zestfully seizes the projectile between her teeth and begins to chomp on it, with unusual aplomb. I have discovered that she was raised in California.

The conversation switches not to sex but to politics.

"Reagan is such a disaster," Carl laments, looking more somber than usual. He wipes his thin lips with the paper towel lying crumpled by his side.

"But his predecessor did not prove to be the magic answer," I reply.

"Well," says Flora, with green elbows on the table, "there are two ways of tackling the present economic situation: watch the fire burn, as Carter did, or pour oil on top of it, like Reagan is suggesting we do. There's just no way he's going to balance the budget by cutting taxes. It's lunacy."

"Funny how Reagan has popularized the idea of demagoguery when he is the biggest demagogue we've ever had," I say.

"It's scary what he's doing to this country," says Carl.

"Incidentally, where's Lily?" I ask.

"She's out for the evening. Oh Albert, I've been meaning to ask you — do you have health insurance?"

"No."

"You should get some; you never know what can happen and hospital bills are horrendous..."

"You're probably right."

"Well, think about it. Seriously. More broccoli?"

Thank you, but I prefer mine to be bright green and with garlic sauce, the way the Siamese prepare it.

\*

# XXI

# AN OLD ACQUAINTANCE

I have filled the car up with regular leaded gas at the station on Connecticut and Nebraska and have trounced down Reno Road to Massachusetts Avenue to Rock Creek Parkway, a sea of white and lavender. A cemetery looms above, the one, if I am not mistaken, adjacent to Montrose Park and Dumbarton Oaks. The flowers are out, there is a delightful scent in the air, and I am now bound for 395.

Should I stop and converse with old Davey Gronket and the Grand Duke of Luxembourg? Know what? The Chrysler Corporation is showing signs of improvement and so am I. So am I. My foot presses the accelerator a tad further to the floor. I pass the Duke Street exit. Hey, Sandra, say hi to the kids and feed them all the steak their little vulture hearts and fangs crave so that they grow up and have ruddy faces and heart problems; and you, nibble on your vegetables. With a little luck your canines will atrophy and your face will extend and you will annex Austria and Czechoslovakia and declare war on Poland, France, England, and the Soviet Union.

I see the signs to Richmond. Hurrah! I yell. A young man is hitchhiking by the sign of the road, I halt the vehicle. He runs towards Balthazar which I slide into reverse. Out of breath he tells me that he is heading for Quantico.

"That's where the Marine Base is?" I ask.

He has short hair and the look of someone who has had much to drink the night before.

"Yeah."

Miles drift by.

"Man," he says, breaking the silence. "I went to this party last night. It was weird."

Were you fed limp, yellow broccoli too?

"This woman comes up to me and asks me: do you recognize me? I look, but the face doesn't ring a bell. Then she plants this big kiss on my lips and says: Harry. I say: you're Harry?? She answers: yeah, Harry Fergusson. But now, I'm Harriet."

"What?"

"I'm telling ya. Weird. She had like real tits — I could feel them — and everything. You could've knocked me down with a toothpick. It was bizarre. The guy should have just accepted that he was gay. Why pretend to be a woman? He or she told me he had his thing cut off and everything. Now could you imagine going around with no dick?"

Did not even keep his balls in a little jar as a souvenir, something at least to show her husband and children when telling tales about when she had been a man?

"Do you remember that passage in *Candide* when Cunégonde, at the time she was still young and beautiful, comes across this man who swears at the misfortune of having been castrated?" I ask.

"Er... No."

"You're probably more familiar with the Bernstein Overture."

"Yeah."

"Could you imagine? Having a gorgeous woman in front of you, willing, and not having the basic hardware?"

"That'd be a real bummer."

"I read recently about this couple in England. At first, it's your typical boy meets girl story. I mean, real boy, real girl."

"I dig."

"Mind you, he's rather effeminate and she's a tomboy and then some. Anyhow, they have children. Two. So far, so good; but then, THEN he gets operated and becomes the woman and she goes through the reverse operation to become the man. I saw photographs and everything."

"Holy shit! That's too weird for me."

"I wonder if he donated his appendage to her?"

"That's a real good question."

The road moves on. The tedium of suburban shopping malls fades into fields and woods. I drop him off at the Quantico exit.

"Hey thanks for the ride, really appreciate it. What's your name?"

"Albert."

"Nice talking to you. I'm Harold."

The trek resumes. I am going down south. With Balthazar. I have never been down south. I am excited. Suddenly I see the oil gauge drop. I pull over to the next exit, get out a rag and check the engine: not a drop of oil in the tank. A gas station is a hundred yards away. I walk over, purchase a can, pour more oil into the car and take off, baffled as to what has happened. Balthazar, after all, is only 14 years old.

An hour or so later I roll into Richmond. A magnificent 19th century railroad station welcomes me. I thought that history had stopped in the South after the Civil War and all that remained were sheds full of people strumming on five dollar guitars and singing the blues.

The building looks abandoned. Will they tear this down too? Simon told me how the station in Syracuse had been transferred to a suburban location, like some airport, thereby defeating one of the system's great advantages: prime downtown location. The Syracuse downtown has a lot of boarded-up buildings, parking lots, and vacant lots with a little historical gem here and there.

Richmond on the other hand seems quite attractive: a lot of row houses, old department stores. People milling around. I follow Jillian's instructions and find her family's townhouse. I park the car and she is there at the door waiting with a big, happy smile, and glowing red hair. The spectacular bosom hidden under a flower pattern blouse is still spectacular.

"Hi! Nice car you got there!"

I notice more of a lilt in her accent than previously.

"Thanks. It used to be my father's."

"Would you like to rest up a bit and see the house?"

The front door is a pleasant old oak brown and features a stained glass motif. We walk up a flight of stairs to the first story. A flowery scent permeates the air. Jillian introduces me to her younger sister, Lizbeth. She is also a redhead with white skin, though slightly taller and a smaller head or perhaps the taller stature conveys that impression.

"Do you like chocolate milkshakes?" She asks. Her nose is slightly more aquiline than Jillian's but her eyes still contain the innocence of childhood. She has not been corrupted by college, adulthood, and the working and job-searching world.

"I love them."

"Good, I'll make you one."

She walks over to the tall refrigerator, takes out ice cream and milk, starts the blender.

Jillian lays her hands on the table. Suddenly I notice a pink blemish on the left.

"What happened?" I ask.

"Oh, I burned myself cooking about a month ago."

A month ago? Then it will probably never heal. Are such details truly important? I look up at the high ceiling.

"This house is beautiful," I tell her.

"Oh, thank you. It was all abandoned when my parents bought it, oh, about seven years ago. You should have seen it back then, a real mess, falling apart, full of rats, but they've really worked hard to remodel it."

"They've done a spectacular job."

There is an indescribable sweetness in the afternoon air. A crimson light is seeping through one of the colored panes of the kitchen window. I feel relaxed as I seldom do in Washington. Almost like closing my eyes. The chocolate shake is superb, with none of the chemical aftertaste so common in the commercial variety. On the wall, facing the sink, hangs a still life, and although one recognizes a tablecloth and a bowl of berries, the strong color patterns, greens, and reds almost give it an abstract quality.

"Did you do that?"

"Oh, a long time ago. It's pretty bad, isn't it?"

"Actually I sort of like it."

When will I have the guts to pull out my palette and easel?

"Thank you. Would you like to go for a walk?" she asks. "The neighborhood is really pretty."

We walk along the brick sidewalks, which time has warped. The Victorian block is a feast for the eye. My head darts in every direction.

"This part of town is called "the Fan" because of the way the streets fan out."

"It's a lot more interesting than your average grid pattern. There's some soul here."

"That's for sure. I love to come out here and jog... By the way, did I tell you that I have a third sister living and studying in Paris right now?"

In every word she speaks there is excitement and melody. I observe her light green skirt which falls slightly below the knee as we walk along.

"I don't think so."

"She's there for a year on an exchange program from the University of North Carolina. She's not a redhead like Lizbeth or myself, but I think she has the same sturdy child-bearing hips. I was thinking about going over to visit. I've never been to Europe and I think it would be exciting. You've lived in France, haven't you?"

"Yes."

"I bet you must miss it."

"A lot, even more when I got here five years ago, at the very beginning. Since my parents don't live there anymore the feeling has become more abstract. I'm unaware, not only of the latest trends but a certain feel in the air, a certain rhythm, certain patterns..."

« A certain *je-ne-sais-quoi*. »

Having said that she giggles blithely, as though speaking French were a subject of great merriment and a tiny bit ridiculous.

"Have you been back to the Hirshhorn?"

"No."

"Isn't that just a wonderful museum? There is a fine, fine museum of art here in Richmond. Perhaps we could go tomorrow? That is if you want to spend the night here."

"Er..."

"There's enough room."

"Sounds good."

Real good.

"What would you like to do tonight? There's a new Indian restaurant not far from here. It's quite good and not too expensive. Maybe we could go see a movie afterwards."

"Couldn't have thought of a more judicious choice myself."

Giggle. There is something mildly devilish about those dark brown eyes.

As the celestial orb begins its downward descent we return to the abode.

"That really is a nice car."

\* \* \*

Breath crooning with curry and various other spices I dare not mention right this second, namely because I do not know their names, we are walking toward the movie theater, Jillian Harmond and I. Although the day's temperature did not exceed 75 degrees, a certain humidity has permeated the air and fumes are rising from the tar. We have opted to see "The Postman Always Rings Twice," starring Jack Nicholson and Jessica Lange.

The room is now dark. Images flicker against the screen. Oh, there's Nicholson, playing a ragamuffin, someone right out of *The Grapes of Wrath*, banging the gas station attendants's wife, like in a work by Henry Miller. She is none other than Jessica Lange with a short, 1930s hairstyle. The mood is bleak, the sex brutal, bestial. It feels odd to be sitting next to a woman you only know platonically while watching scenes of promiscuity. There seems to be a sort of a gap. The fact that infidelity is involved makes it worse. And more titillating.

Jillian's eyes are riveted to the screen while mine are peering at her left shoulder. I slide my arm on the armrest and then around her shoulder. Eyes half shut, she turns her head towards mine and it is not to converse. I near mine. These are the types of moment you wish would last forever, the half second *before*. Soon our tongues are playing a drowsy game of cat and mouse. She is a fantastic kisser and the aroma of her skin stirs something deep inside of me. It is more than an aroma, it is a liqueur. I am beginning to understand the power of the redhead. The film, on the other hand, has ceased to inspire us, it seems a violent and meaningless collage. Perhaps it would be better in black and white, the color only adds to the obscenity.

"Do you like it?" she whispers.

"Not a whole lot."

"Let's get out of here."

"Gladly."

Michael Kent

We walk slowly toward a club featuring local folk artists and then back to the handsome Victorian abode. We hear noises downstairs.

"Oh that must be my parents. I guess they're back from Washington."

I am introduced to Guy and Sharon, two enthusiastic people excited by their trip to the capital. She looks somewhat like a schoolteacher, which she is, and he looks like a minister, which he is.

"Sorry kids," the father says after a few minutes, "but we're bushed so we're going to have to say goodnight."

Alone in the living room, Jillian and I resume our movie-watching activity.

"Gosh, you northern boys are awfully fast."

It sounds like something one would say at a fraternity party. I stare down at Jillian and cannot help but think that she has a funny looking nose.

"No point in wasting time."

My hand wanders up her back. The skin is soft until I reach a hurdle between the shoulder blades. My fingers feel the terrain and snap it off.

"Boy, that was skillful," she whispers.

"It's called experience."

Her breathing is getting harder and her bed is quite big enough to fit four, but it is alone that I sleep in it. Indeed, she retires to her sister's chamber.

Until fairly late the following morning. I can hear people moving about on the other side of the door. When I get up to brush my teeth an ugly surprise awaits: a contact lens case. I scratch the back of my head. Is this the right woman for me? How many more imperfections await? I do wear glasses myself; I should not be too judgmental. I think I have inherited most of my father's insanity and then some.

A few minutes later I find out to my great shame that Lizbeth is the short-sighted one in the family. Lizbeth who is sitting on her bed, playing the slide guitar. The steel bottle-neck rides up and down the frets. I am propelled to 1972, the first time I saw John Lennon on French television, playing an acoustic version of "Attica State" — which ended up on the "Sometime in New York City" with a battalion of instruments choking the original power and simplicity.

"Oh that's John Lennon?" my mother said.

"You know him?" I asked, bewildered.

"Oh, come on, I know I'm not your generation but I do know a few things. He was one of the Beatles."

The Beatles. It sounded magical.

"Really?"

"Yes. He's the one who posed in the nude with that Japanese wife of his."

Mother did not approve of such things. But I thought it was cool.

After a cozy, relaxed, sun-drenched brunch in central Richmond, Jillian and I drive over to the Edgar Allan Poe house.

"My, you're pretty frisky behind that wheel! Is that the Massachusetts or the French?"

"It's the Nostran. Do you see the Poe house anywhere?"

"That's it over there. Yeah, I know, it's no House of the Seven Gables."

It is a small, ancient stone structure; not unlike a lock keeper's dwelling, outside which an engraved raven stands guard.

"Anyone home?" Jillian yells in one of the windows. This woman is feisty. If there were wolves inside, she would see it as an incentive to go in.

"Hm, it looks abandoned. Come and see."

"Not much here, except that it would be a cool place to spend the summer."

"But pretty dark, don't you think? I believe there's been some talk of restoring it. We'll have to return in a couple of years."

"Fine by me."

"But this hill here is also really famous."

"Is it?"

"Oh, yes."

I like the way she says 'oh, yes.' Both hopeful and feminine. We climb to the top of the grassy mound, to fall smack dab in the middle of a wedding ceremony.

"Oh it's the Patrick Henry Church. Two men got married here a month ago," says Jillian.

*"O tempora, o mores."*

"Pretty strange, eh? I mean, assuming they are in love, why should two men want to marry?"

"To make it easy on the children?"

She laughs out loud.

"Ooooh, can you imagine?"

Her face twists into a horrifying frown. I notice that she has no hair at the beginning of the temples.

Our next stop is the Fine Arts Gallery, a modern angular brick structure featuring the Fabergé egg collection. The treasures of czarist Russia in the capital of the Old South. I am holding the hand with a thumb hiding the pink burn mark that will never disappear. When we exit, the morning sunshine has been replaced by clouds and humidity. Jillian starts singing "Heartbreak Hotel."

"I think I must be returning to Washington. I'm working tomorrow. Er... why don't you come up and visit sometime?"

"That would be great! Oh, I'm so glad you made it down here. I had a fabulous time!"

Regardless of the blemish, the lack of hair on the temples, and what some would deem to be an oversized derrière, she is intelligent and, ah, fragrant. My nostrils are still quivering. She is also very sweet, and I am beginning to think that that is sometimes the greatest aphrodisiac. Kindness... and my body is all astir. If only Claire could have comprehended that! I am halfway to Washington when it dawns on me I should have told my Southern belle that I had a fabulous weekend too. My mind unpredictably switches to *Manon Lescaut*. I am about halfway through. The Chevalier des Grières must really be thunderstruck to stay with such a woman.

When I arrive in Washington the sky is like the blackish blue ink I have recently bought for my fountain pen.

\*

# XXII

# ON WINDOWS

A nother day working without windows, not knowing if a new ice age has hit or the asphalt has turned to slush; pale green plastic-coated, washable walls like the material with which I used to cover my textbooks in grade school; white tubes of light buzzing on the ceiling; shuffling mail around. But now I have been officiously appointed to supervise the others. Jay Kruger trusts me.

"Not that box, buddy... let me see... Give that to me, better that I take care of it."

I am no longer in the middle of international events, but away from book-peddling and page-numbering, tiptoeing up the rungs of a growing company that will change the way America thinks of telephones. La-la-la.

"You know, I'm sort of a psychologist," says George, my African-American colleague, as I return from the soda machine with a frothing can of ginger ale. "And I think that the two of you would be a perfect match."

"Oh, come on!" says Sarah, the woman with the speech impediment.

I look at her. She flashes a knowing smile. I smile back through the beard she thinks I should shave while my mind shuffles back to Richmond, Jillian, and then, Claire. Stop mind, stop. And what is the matter with you, heart? Oh, Claire, what fool are you torturing now? The Duke of Luxembourg? Poor lad, I envy him not. Or have you decided to follow your lovely body and become a full-fledged adult?

Jillian is ready to give. In college I had no one. A hint or a prelude perhaps, like a ham sandwich without the ham. No mustard even. As bad as the real world is, I do not miss the academic fortress, the learning no-man's-land for a second; still, I do not wish my intellectual or at least writing endeavors to fade with UWS. Bukowski certainly tired of the mail room. Even if he wrote some good poetry in the process.

My God, my article! How long has it been since I posted it? Two weeks? I take a break from my envelopes and dial the Alexandria Gazette's newsroom number. My stomach is pregnant with apprehension. The same cranky woman answers.

"The article on the Uruguay sculptor? Yeah, it's been published."

WHAT?!!! AAAAAAAAAAAAAAAAAAAAAAAHH!!! The asinine tone sounds more melodious than Schubert.

"Oh, it has? Could you mail me a copy?"

Mrs. Bartok, please.

"Sure; we have your address, don't we?"

No, I just mail manuscripts out to the wind.

"And... Will I get paid for it?"

"We can give you fifteen dollars, if you want. That's the authorized ceiling."

If you want? What is this? Thanks also for letting me know. BUT, I HAVE BEEN PUBLISHED.

"Fine."

\*　\*　\*

"Now you can say you're a professional writer," Flora responds with a big encouraging and ever toothy smile as I come home that evening. With a bottle of Mouton Cadet. Can't wait to hear that cork pop.

"That's good, Albert," adds Carl from his desk up the stairs.

I call my mother. Too bad if the rates go down even further at 11 post meridiem.

"You had an article published? Oh, darling, I'm so proud of you, but, listen, I've got news for you."

"You do?"

My face twists. Suddenly, I fear the worst.

"Your father is coming back tomorrow."

"What? He is?!"

"Yes! The doctors have never seen such a case. It's almost like a miracle. Isn't that amazing? Who would have ever believed it? Let's just hope he doesn't go back to his old tricks... But he's been so sweet recently, I can hardly recognize him."

"That's good to know. Has he read my letters?"

"Oh, sure. You know how he loves you in his own mad way. He always asks about you. Still enjoying your new living quarters?"

"Pretty much."

I look down at my cot, the marble table which split into two shortly after the move but that I have glued back together in the basement. Flora is leery as to the long-term consequences, picturing the marble collapsing, scratching, and denting the, her, parquet floor.

"I bet you're glad to be away from that Gronket or whatever character. I can still hear him telling me about the sums of money you owed him for the electricity or the telephone... Such ridiculous sums; and innocent me thinking Americans were above such petty matters."

I shake my head.

"Speaking of money, how are matters financially on your side?"

"They seem to be coming along. Of course, there's the mortgage and the horrible taxes of this bloody state... Oh I wish I could just sell this house and find an apartment or a condo somewhere."

"And be uprooted all over again?"

"I have no roots here. I'm not an American; I would like a place by the sea though. I just love to get up in the morning and look out the window; I get this sense of freedom. When are you coming to visit?"

"Pretty soon, hopefully."

"Oh, do you have to say things like 'hopefully?' It's not even a real word. Are you still in that mail room?"

"Yes."

"That's not leading anywhere. Why don't you just pack it up and come back to Stone Harbor? It gets awfully lonely up here and there's plenty of room."

"But what kind of job is there for me?"

"I suppose, but at least you can come and visit... I feel I have no family anymore. Your brother is never anywhere to be found... Maybe try to give him a call at 11, maybe he'll be there, you never can tell."

"Okay. You should come down to Washington."

"With your father and all? No, I don't think that would work out too well. Anyhow, it's nice of you to call your old Mum and I am delighted about the article. Send me a copy when you get it."

"Definitely. Goodbye, Mama."

I replace the receiver on the hook, look out my window and see a ray of sunshine and the gutter's shadow carving a crescent, a smile. The sun is setting. Verlaine, lend me a word; Turner, where is your palette? On the windowsill lies my copy of *Manon Lescaut*, browned by the years in the box up in the attic. Attics are indeed the house's soul. I have about ten pages to go before the final dénouement.

Time to wash. I leave my small room, walk through the narrow corridor through Flora and Carl's diminutive love-nest through which I gain access to the shower. "My" bathroom, facing the stairs, has the bath, "theirs" has the shower. They let me use it, and I would let them use mine except that they have not expressed any interest. Strange, baths can be much more of a meditative and fulfilling experience. Of course, they do take longer and generally require more water.

Before turning on the faucets, I caress the leaves of the large locust tree which is prospering over the tiles. When you exit the shower you feel you are in a jungle. Back in the Garden of Eden. The eye and nature become suddenly flooded with chlorophyll — a synesthesia, complemented by the pines in the back yard, which at certain times of day prevent the sun from reaching the back of the house.

As I am drying my hair with the towel, vigorously, the telephone rings. Twice, three times.

"IT'S FOR YOU, ALBERT," yells Carl from downstairs.

"THANK YOU. Hello?"

THE ABOVE CAN BE READ FROM LEFT TO RIGHT AND FROM RIGHT TO LEFT.

"Oh, hi! It's me, Jillian. I got your letter and the cartoon. It was so funny! That man who looks right and left a couple of times and then disappears into his suit with his head. Goodness, I laughed out loud. My parents must think I'm crazy."

"How are they?"

"Just fine and so is Lizbeth, who says hello. Listen, I'm supposed to visit a couple of friends up in Washington next weekend; so, maybe that would be a good time to get together?"

Her voice becomes lower, more earnest.

"Absolutely."

I hang up the phone, scratch the back of my head. Can a burn mark last forever? I think I shall save Manon for tonight, after I talk to Simon. Time to breathe the outside air and go for a long promenade; just walk on until I am too tired to move another muscle and return on one of the Connecticut Avenue buses or hitchhike; there might be a good film showing down at Dupont Circle.

It must have rained; the air is cool and fragrant with the smell of wet leaves. The neighbor across the street waves, a nice old man with a full head of white hair and eyeglasses, always ready to lend a tool or a piece of advice. My legs feel strong.

My God, I have been published. In a real newspaper, in the real world. Published. Aah. How sweet the sound. As the man who loved women remarked in the eponymous film. The magic of seeing your name in print. A by-line. Music. Bugles. Tympani. Notes like hatchets or balls of hail. Like baby icebergs clinking in a vat of single-malt scotch. Gulan has pointed me in the right direction. A magnolia bush sprinkles a little water on my forehead. The first mercury vapor lamps have started to glow.

**THE END**

# ABOUT THE AUTHOR

B orn 1958, Boulogne-Billancourt, France, writer, artist, musician, published Les Maléfices du fardeau d'Atlas, his first book of poetry in 1985. He has written five novels, including THE BIG JIGGETY (Xlibris, 2005) and POP THE PLUG (Xlibris 2012). Also, his verse has been published in The Poet's Domain. His short stories and, on occasion, art work, have found a niche in Happy, Kinesis, The Quill, The Urban Age, Voie Express USA, The Threshold, The Writer's Round Table and Moscow's renowned Inostrania Literatura (next to T.C. Boyle). Writing in both English and French, his works have been translated into Spanish and Russian. Aside from selling books and the occasional painting (see Flickr/ TheBigJiggety). he currently earns a living in Washington, DC as a French-English interpreter/translator and likes to sing and play old rock & roll with a few friends (see YouTube: BigJiggety).

Printed in the United States
By Bookmasters